I0642144

Thomas Scott

Lyric Poems

Devotional and Moral

Thomas Scott

Lyric Poems
Devotional and Moral

ISBN/EAN: 9783742814388

Manufactured in Europe, USA, Canada, Australia, Japa

Cover: Foto ©Andreas Hilbeck / pixelio.de

Manufactured and distributed by brebook publishing software
(www.brebook.com)

Thomas Scott

Lyric Poems

LYRIC POEMS,

DEVOTIONAL

AND

MORAL.

By THOMAS SCOTT.

—— DEO DATE CARMINA DIGNA.

BUCHAN.

LONDON:

PRINTED FOR JAMES BUCKLAND, AT THE
BUCK, IN PATER-NOSTER ROW.
MDCCLXXIII.

PREFACE.

THE Author of the following pieces aimed, in the choice and arrangement of their several subjects, to form a kind of little poetical system of piety and morals. The work opens with natural religion. Thence it proceeds to the mission of Jesus Christ, his sufferings, his exaltation, and the propagation of his doctrine. Next is the call to repentance, the nature and blessedness of a christian life, and the entrance into it. These topics are succeeded by the various branches of devotion: after which are ranked the moral duties personal and social, the happy end of a sincere christian, and the coming of Jesus Christ to finish his mediatorial kingdom by the general judgment. The whole is closed with a description of the illustrious times, when, by means of the everlasting gospel, *the earth shall be full of the knowlege of the Lord as the waters cover the sea* [a].

---

[a] If. xi. 9.

The

PREFACE.

The novelty of fuch a plan, in verfe, will, perhaps, be a recommendation of it : If, however, verfe be thought too light and fuperficial for religious inftruction, let the royal pfalmift ftand forth and wipe off the reproach.

That thefe poems might not pall the ear, variety of metre was adopted : and that they might fatisfy the underftanding, great care has been employed to deduce the fentiments from fcripture, reafon, or experience. The fcripture fentiments are marked with reference letters ; and the correfponding texts appear in the bottom margin.

In hope, therefore, of affifting well-difpofed minds, in their nobleft pleafures and improvements ; the writer hazards the publication of this fmall performance.

CON-

CONTENTS.

CONTENTS.

7

CONTENTS.

LXXXI. Re-

CONTENTS.

LYRIC

A new double Tune,

Made for Hymn XII, by Mr. Wm. Cole of Colchester.

Thou Son of God, virtue's immortal friend,

With Glo-ry crown'd in worlds on high;

Ne'er shall thy vast do-minion know its end,

Till Time and Death and Nature die. Till

Time and Death and Nature die.

Terreftrial Thrones, and high celeftial Powers,
Obey thy all-commanding Nod.
Hell trembles; and with all her Princes cow'rs
Beneath the terror of thy Rod.

A Mortal once, 'mong sinful mortals born,   A lowly Virgin gave thee Birth: No Palace did thy natal Hour adore, No festal welcome thee on Earth.

Thy infant Limbs the cradling manger knew;
Thy Youth was in a Cottage train'd.
Poor and defpif'd thy Years to manhood grew;
In manhood poor, a man difdain'd.

In perils oft, in painful toils and grief,
Thy days were fpent to blefs mankind;
To give the wounded heart divine relief,
And heav'nly Vifion to the blind.

To call the wand'ring in the darkfome road
Of Ignorance, and Sin, and Death;
To charm them back to Virtue, Peace, and God,
Employ'd each moment of thy Breath.

At length, to finifh great Redemption's plan,
In Duty to his Father's Will;
Extended on a Crofs, the wondrous man
Expires —— his mercy to fulfill.

(Sing the following Stanza to the firft Tune.)

Loud Anthems hail'd thee to thy Father's throne,
Virtue ftill occupies thy Care.
Let the whole Earth thy golden Scepter own,
Let the whole Earth thy Blefsings fhare.

LYRIC POEMS,

DEVOTIONAL AND MORAL.

I.

G O D.

O COULD I fweep the lyre, like Ifrael's King,
    And with his voice in lofty numbers fing;
No far-fam'd hero fhould infpire my ftrain,
Nor fabled Jove the mighty verfe fuftain.
Thy acts, Jehovah, be my fong's high ftory,
Thy peerlefs name, and thy unbounded glory.

B   Sole

Sole unbegotten *, independent Pow'r,
Years are but moments, ages but an hour
To thee: Ere time had ſtarted from his goal,
Thy eſſence was: When time ſhall ceaſe to roll
His flaming orbs, thy eſſence, ſtill abiding,
Defies decay; in its own ſtrength confiding.

Vaſt ſource of being, at thy potent word
Creation's wonders roſe, and hail'd thee Lord.
The changing moon and the all-foſt'ring ſun
Their functions know, and in thy circles run.
Earth her appointed ſtation holds: While Ocean,
Aw'd by thy limits, curbs his wild commotion.

Great Sultan, Majeſty Supreme, what awe
Surrounds thy throne and guards thy holy law!
Thy law is holy; to the rebel, woe:
Thy law is good; what peace the duteous know!
Celeſtial worlds obey; in bliſs abounding:
Thou Earth, obey; his ſeat with odes ſurrounding.

---

* By this term the ancient writers of the Chriſtian church
expreſſed the *ſelf-exiſtence* of the Supreme Being.　See Dr.
Scott's edition of Bailey's Dictionary, Article UNBEGOT-
TEN.

　　　　　　　　　　　　　　Father

Father of men, thy love what meafures bound ?
Whofe fulnefs overflows this finning ground :
Thy clouds effufe their alms, the fountains flow,
The fields rejoice, the trees with fruitage glow.
But man, thy image in his foul fuftaining,
Lives on thy bounty thanklefs and complaining.

Where fhall the wicked flee ? What darknefs fhade
Guilt, from thofe eyes whofe beams the foul pervade ?
Where can the righteous weep, from thee conceal'd,
Thy ear not hearing, nor thy arm reveal'd ?
Myfterious Prefence ! all thy works exploring :
Knowledge fublime ! above all finite foaring.

✳✳✳✳✳✳✳✳✳✳✳✳✳✳✳✳✳✳✳✳✳✳✳✳✳✳✳✳✳✳✳✳✳✳✳✳

II.

MANIFESTATION OF GOD IN THE HEAVENS.

[a]THE firmament's ftupendous frame,
Where worlds on worlds in order flame,
In order wheel their azure rounds,
Thy grandeur, mighty God, refounds.

---

[a] See Pfalm xix.

Day rolling after day difplays
Thy providence, with lofty praife.
In fhadowy robe night rides along,
And ecchoes loud the lafting fong.

Their univerfal voice demands
Attention, from all reafon's lands.
To every clime their fpeech is known,
Let every clime thy wonders own.

All in majeftic fplendor bright,
Thy pow'rful minifter of light,
Forth from his eaftern palace, gay,
Springs out ; to fhed the vital ray.

Gay as a youth, in glowing bloom,
Forth iffues from his fpoufal room ;
Strong as a champion racer's force,
He rufhes to his mighty courfe.

With fwift career, from heav'n's extreme
To heav'n's remoteft end, his beam
Illumes, O earth, thy joyous feat;
And warms all nature with his heat.

III.

INVITATION TO WORSHIP GOD.

GREAT Spirit, underftanding's king,
  Reafon and truth muft join to bring
Worfhip, which may prefume to meet
Acceptance at thy holy feat.

The lifted hand, the bending knee,
Is but vain homage, Lord, to thee:
In vain our lips the hymn prolong,
The heart a ftranger to the fong.

Can rites, and forms, and flaming zeal
The breaches of thy mandates heal?
Or faft and penance reconcile
Thy juftice, and obtain thy fmile? [a]

A foul devout, a confcience clean,
And goodnefs in each focial fcene,
To thee a nobler off'ring yield,
Than Sheba's * groves or Sharon's † field-;

-----

[a] Ifaiah LVIII. 5, 7.

 * Arabia the Happy, famous for its gold and frank-incenfe.

 † A large extent of plains round about Joppa and Lydda, all rich pafture land.

     Than

Than floods of oil, and floods of wine,
Ten thoufand rolling to thy fhrine :
Or than, if to thy altar led,
A firft-born fon, the victim, bled [a].

Kneel, kneel, ye tribes of human frame,
Kneel; and adore the Maker's name.
Let every clime the fun goes round,
In every tongue his glory found.

The beftial clans, which round you graze,
With dumb devotion act his praife;
Who gave you pow'rs to them unknown ?
Speech is your wondrous boaft alone.

In you there lives, what ne'er fhall die,
A free-born, thinking energy ;
Fafhion'd and furnifh'd to fulfill
Reafon's high law, your Father's will [b].

How long revolting, will ye rove
From hill to hill, from grove to grove ?
And, mad with fuperftition, fear
Gods which can neither fee nor hear [c].

---

[a] Micah vi. 6—8.   [b] Job xxxii. 8. xxxv. 10, 11.
[c] Pfalm cxv. 6—8.

O come,

O come, and feek your father's face,
His anger fear, his love embrace;
Who in the world beyond the grave,
Has pow'r to kill and pow'r to fave.

IV.

PRAISE TO THE CREATOR.

AWAKE, my glory [a], awake [b];
    O found his honours abroad.
Before the mountains were born
    He was; eternity's God [c].

[d] The fun he kindled; he fow'd
    The blue expanfion with ftars.
The earth he founded [e]; he made
    The fea, and prifon'd with bars [f].

---

[a] The tongue.   [b] Pfalm LVII. 8.   [c] Pfalm XC. 2.
[d] Genef. I.   [e] Pfalm XXIV. 2. Job XXXVIII. 4, 6.
[f] Job XXXVIII. 8, 10.

          The

The winds he balanc'd; he gave
  The cloud his ruling command,
To dart the arrows [a] of heav'n,
  With rain to fatten the land [b].

He form'd his image the laft,
  Above all creatures beneath :
Of clay the body he wrought,
  The foul infus'd with his breath [c].

O man, half angel in mind [d],
  O mortal, fprung from the duft,
Thy Maker's glories adore,
  Thy Maker's clemency truft.

Awake, my glory, awake;
  O found his honours abroad.
Before the mountains were born
  He was; eternity's God.

---

[a] Lightning. [b] Job xxviii. 25, 26. Pfalm xviii. 14.
[c] Gen. i. 26—30. ii. 7.   [d] Pfalm viii. 5—8.

V.

THE SANCTITY OF GOD.

O Sanctity, whose cloudless day
    Abhors pollution's smallest stain [a];
How shall a worm that dwells in clay,
    One moment in thy view remain?

Ah! shall a wretch deform'd with sin,
    In all his pow'rs of soul defil'd,
Not blush to claim his origin
    From thee, and boast himself thy child?

Never, O never, thy decrees
    This loathsom leprosy infus'd.
Myself let in the dire disease,
    Myself my reas'ning self abus'd [b].

Passions, in giddy youth unrein'd,
    With years to headstrong habit grew:
And sin still fresh dominion gain'd,
    Old crime augmenting still with new.

-----

[a] 1 John i. 5.   [b] Ecclef. vii. 29.

Self-

Self-ruin'd, helpless ; Lord, with thee
   Help lives in opulent abode.
Almighty Mercy calls " by me
   " Songs of falvation are beftow'd."

O, as in fome pellucid ftream
   We love to view the pictur'd fky ;
My foul might yield, tho' faint the beam,
   An image of thy purity !

VI.

DIVINE BENEVOLENCE.

IN fhadow black as night,
   With fcarce one feeble ray
Of nature's dim expiring light,
   The nations loft their way.

Like foolifh fheep we ftray'd,
   All from the Maker's fold:
Each, by his fev'ral fin betray'd,
   His fev'ral path would hold [a].

[a] Ifaiah LIII. 6.

Blind,

Blind, headlong every one
   To the fame ruin ran.
Th' Almighty Father, from his throne,
   Beheld his creature man.

His wilder'd human race
   The Father's pity won:
Forth from the bofom of his grace
   He fent his firft-born fon [a].

Benevolent he came,
   The meffenger of love [b];
Debafing to a mortal frame
   His godlike form above [c].

With gentle voice hè cries,
   " Sinners my yoke receive:
" Light is my yoke, and life the prize
   " I to the yielding give [d]."

Truth fpreads her golden wings,
   With the glad news fhe flew;
Salvation through the world fhe brings
   To Gentile and to Jew.

---

[a] John III. 16, 17. Coloff. I. 15.   [b] John I. 16, 17.
[c] John III. 13. VI. 62. Philipp. II. 6—8.
[d] Matt. XI. 28—30.

O mercy

O mercy fweet and high,
  Above our loftieft praife :
Ye noble natives of the fky,
  Your nobleft anthems raife.

VII.

JESUS CHRIST.

SAGES of letter'd Greece and Rome,
  Ev'n thou * by feign'd Apollo's doom
Announced wifeft of mankind,
Withdraw your thinly-fcatter'd rays ;
Before the broad o'erpow'ring blaze
Of the fupreme eternal mind.

---

* Socrates, pronounced by the oracle at Delphi the
wifeft among men.

Mercy's

Mercy's great year [a], in heav'n inroll'd,
By feers fucceeding feers foretold [b],
   Was now with folemn pomp unfeal'd.
Light of the world [c] Meſſiah came,
In his almighty Father's name,
   And immortality reveal'd [d].

Fill'd with his Father's ſtrength he taught;
The dumb in rapture ſpeak their thought,
   The lame man bounding like the roe:
The blind look up to heav'n, ſtern death
Reſigns its ſpoil, and from his breath
   Fierce Demons ſhrink to ſhades below [e].

O works of pow'r, O works of love,
Ethereal embaſſage to prove,
   That ev'ry riſing doubt control;
Earneſt of love and pow'r more ſtrong,
Which to the ſon of God belong,
   To heal the miferies of the ſoul.

---

[a] Iſaiah LXI. 1—3.   Luke IV. 16—21.
[b] Luke I. 68—70.   [c] John VIII. 12.
[d] 2 Tim. I. 10.   [e] Luke VIII. 32.

Great

Great Prophet, Saviour, worthy thou
That every knee in homage bow,
   From every mouth thy praife fhould flow:
All thy commands are mild and juft,
Thy promife, faithful to our truft,
   Will pardon, peace, and heav'n beftow.

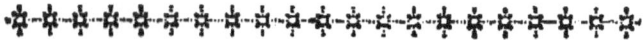

VIII.

JEWISH AND CHRISTIAN RELIGION
COMPARED.

'TWAS not to bathe in Jordan's flood,
   Nor touch nor tafte precifely pure,
Nor holy wafte of brutal blood,
   Nor faft fevere nor look demure,

That could the God of Ifrael pleafe;
   When Amram's fon his precepts taught,
And by fuch myftic rites as thefe,
   Labour'd to moralize the thought.

At

At length the fon of God appears,
  Truth drops her emblematic drefs.
A nobler form religion wears,
  Adorn'd with fimple holinefs.

No more let zeal for mode and rite
  The name of fanctity affume.
Leave to the folemn hypocrite,
  Thefe trappings of adult'rous Rome.

Sacred to God be all within ;
  From guile, from bafe affections free :
So his high friendfhip thou fhalt win,
  And beatific vifion fee.

IX.

THE COMPASSION OF
JESUS CHRIST.

YE Angel Forms, look down; and fee
    A fcene of ftrange diftrefs below :
Behold divine humanity
  Diffolv'd in fympathetic woe.

Lo,

Lo, on high Olivet he ſtands,

   Salem's proud tow'rs in proſpect riſe:
His bowels yearn, he ſpreads his hands,
   Compaſſion guſhing from his eyes:

" O Salem, my prophetic view
   " Thy mighty miſeries ſurveys;
" Vengeance, to thy rebellions due,
   " Unknown in paſt and future days.

" What labours have I ſhunn'd, for thee?
   " What pow'rs of ſuaſion left untry'd,
" Thy children to allure to me,
   " And in a Saviour's ſhadow hide?

" So when the falcon ſails above,
   " The parent hen, with tender cry,
" Under her guardian wing of love
   " Collects her infant progeny.

" But ah! ye would not—O ye blind!
   (He ſaid, and heav'd a deeper ſigh)
" Your temple is to flames conſign'd;
   " The dark predeſtin'd hour is nigh ᵃ.

ᵃ Matt. xxiii. 37, &c.   Luke xix. 41—44.

Bleſt Jeſus, in thy feeling heart
  For me, a ſinner, ſpare one place.
I would be thine—O yield a part
  To me, in thy redeeming grace.

X.

THE AGONY OF JESUS CHRIST.

BRING me, O bring me where thy mournful
    ſhade,
  Thou fam'd Gethſemane [a], ſuch woe conceal'd ;
As Time had never in his courſe ſurvey'd,
  Nor Time's old annals ever yet reveal'd.

Who there in agony of ſorrow lies ?
  From all his pores the ſanguine currents run [b]:
I hear his groans, I hear his bitter cries :
  'Tis holy Jeſus, God's redeeming ſon.

---

[a] Matt. xxvi. 36—44. [b] Luke xxiv. 44. Heb. v. 7.

Lo, on the ground he falls : he falls again :
   Again he falls—in vehemence of pray'r :
" Father, if poſſible, thy hand refrain,
    " Far from my lip this dreadful chalice bear.

" But if the wiſdom of thy good decree
    " Will'd thus to ſave loſt man ; if thus alone,
" Thy injur'd name is honour'd beſt ; in me
    " *Thy* will be finiſh'd, Father, not *my own.*"

Ye ſtarry fires, which o'er his ſorrows blaz'd,
   Could you in all your nightly journies find
Compaſſion ſo divine, devotion rais'd
   So high, and reſignation ſo reſign'd ?

XI.

HIS APPREHENSION.

THE traitor comes, with ruffian crew:
    " Good mafter, hail," the traitor cries,
Then gives the fignal kifs ; anew
    The traitor calls, " hold faft your prize ª."

Whither ye rude, unhallow'd hands,
    My Lord, my Saviour, will ye bear ?
O muft the prince of life thefe bands
    Of vileft ignominy wear ᵇ ?

He muft; ev'n he, whofe voice could bring
    His father's legions down to earth ;
Ten thoufand thoufand on the wing,
    To guard his life who fang his birth.

ª Matt. xxvi. 48, 49. Mark xiv. 44.
ᵇ John xviii. 12.

He

He muſt; all reſcue hc declines:
     " Elſe oracles in vain foretell
" Eternal wiſdom's great deſigns,
     " To ſave a guilty world from hell [a]."

Behold, the willing victim goes,
    As a meek lamb to ſlaughter led [b]:
What noble fortitude he ſhews!
    His look, how calm! erect, his head!

O Jeſus, ſhould thy cauſe require
    My blood its heav'n-born truth to ſeal;
Me, in that trying day, inſpire
    With thy divinely-glowing zeal.

----

[a] Matt. xxvi. 53, 54.   [b] Iſaiah liii. 7.

XII.

HIS CONDEMNATION AND CRUCIFIXION.

BOUND in a malefactor's chains [a]
    Malice his innocence arraigns;
Malice her venom'd fpittle throws,
Fierce Malice deals her fierceft blows [b].

With crown of thorns his temples bleed,
With cruel ftripes his back is flea'd [c],
Behold the man [d]—" The crofs," they call [e],
" The crofs," and rend the judgement hall [e].

What evil has he wrought ? " Away,
" Barabbas fave [f], this fellow [g] flay."
Bloody and faint he bears along
His crofs, amidft a hooting throng.

---

[a] John xviii. 24.   [b] Matt. xxvi. 59—61, 67.
[c] Matt. xxvii. 26, 29, 30.   [d] John xix. 4, 5.
[e] John xix. 6. Luke xxiii. 21—23.
[f] Matt. xxvii. 21—23.   [g] Luke xxiii. 2.

        Incon-

Inconftant throng ! the day before
Heard your wide mouths *hofannas* roar :
" *Meffiah, king,*" with fhoutings loud
You hail'd him [a].   O inconftant crowd !

Ingrates ! where fhall your lame, your blind,
Your fick another healer find ?
Whence fhall another Jefus come,
To guide you to his father's home [b] ?

Ah ! they have nail'd him to the tree,
Between the fons of infamy [c].
And now the fcornful head they fhake
And now th' infulting jeft they break [d].

But oh ! what tongue his grief can tell,
When on his foul that darknefs fell ?
" My God, my God and Father, why
" By thee forfaken muft I die [e] ?"

   Flow, flow my tears, in torrents flow ;
My fins, dear Lord, wrought all thy woe.
Help my weak faith, and with thy pow'r
Uphold me in temptation's hour.

---

[a] Matt. xxi. 8, 9.   [b] John xiv. 2, 3.
[c] Ifaiah liii. 12.   Matt. xxvii. 38.
[d] Matt. xxvii. 39, 40.   [e] Matt. xxvii. 46.

XIII.

GLORYING IN THE CROSS
OF CHRIST.

THE nail, the fpear, the fhaming tree
    I make my boafted theme [a].
On Calvary's mount, O God, I fee
    Thy pow'r and wifdom beam [b].

There is my Saviour's miffion read
    In characters of blood,
The Chrift the fon of God ; he bled
    To make his title good [c].

Illuftrious act of duty, paid
    To his great Father's will [d] !
Virtue, in torments, undifmay'd
    Does it's high work fulfill.

---

[a] Gal. vi. 14.   [b] i Corinth. i. 24.   [c] Matt. xxvi.
6;—67.   Jchn xix. 7.   i Tim. vi. 13.   oh. xviii. 37.
[d] Philip. ii. 8,

Awful

Awful atonement [a]! now with smiles
   Justice the pardon gives;
When to himself God reconciles
   The sinner who believes.

Faith at the crofs new vigour feels
   (There hope and peace begin)
Subdues my fears, my sorrow heals,
   And triumphs o'er my sin [b].

Let scorners mock and die [c]; while those
   Who love the Saviour's name,
With firm contempt their scorn oppose,
   And his salvation claim [d].

---

[a] Dan. ix. 24.   Rom. iii. 25, 26.   2 Cor. v. 19.
[b] Gal. ii. 20.   [c] Acts xiii. 41.   [d] 2 Tim. iv. 8.

XIV.

HIS RESURRECTION AND ASCENSION.

TREMBLING earth gave awful fign;
>   hallelujah.

Down from heav'n a form divine
>   hallelujah.

Flafh'd; the lightning of his look
>   hallelujah.

Terror in the foldiers ftrook [a].
>   hallelujah.

Angel, roll the rock away;
Death yield up thy mighty prey:
See ! He rifes from the tomb,
Glowing with immortal bloom.

'Tis the Saviour ! Angel, raife
Fame's eternal trump of praife:
Let the world's remoteft bound
Hear the joy-infpiring found.

---

[a] Matt. xxviii. 1—4.

B2   Shout,

Shout, ye faints, in rapt'rous fong,
Let the ftrains be fweet and ftrong:
Shout the fon of God, this morn
From his fepulchre new-born.

Hail, victorious Jefu, hail;
On thy cloud of glory fail [a]
In long triumph through the fky,
Up to waiting worlds on high.

Heav'n difplays her portals wide,
Glorious hero, through them ride;
King of glory, mount the throne,
Thy great father's and thy own [b].

Pow'rs of heav'n, Seraphic Fires,
Sing, and fweep your golden lyres:
Sons of men, in humbler ftrain,
Sing your mighty Saviour's reign.

---

[a] Acts I. 9, 10.　　[b] Revel. III. 21.

Ev'ry

Ev'ry note with wonders fwell,
Sin o'erthrown and captiv'd hell:
Where is hell's once dreaded king?
Where, O Death, thy mortal fting [a] *?*

XV.

HIS LOWLY AND EXALTED STATE COMPARED.

THOU Son of God, virtue's immortal friend,
 With glory crown'd in worlds on high [b];
Ne'er fhall thy vaft dominion know its end,
 Till time and death and nature die [c].

Terreftrial thrones and empyrean [d] Pow'rs
 Obey thy all commanding nod [e]:
Hell trembles, and with all her princes cow'rs
 Beneath the terror of thy rod [f].

---

[a] 1 Corinth. xv. 55—57.   [b] Heb. ii. 9.
[c] Dan. vii. 13, 14.   1 Corinth. xv. 24—28.
[d] *Celeftial,* or *heavenly.*   [e] Ephef. i. 20, 21.
Philip. ii. 9—11.   [f] Revel. i. 18.

A mortal

A mortal once, 'mong finful mortals born,
 A lowly virgin gave thee birth.
No palace did thy natal hour adorn,
 No feftal welcome thee on earth.

Thy infant limbs the cradling manger knew,
 Thy youth was in a cottage train'd :
Poor and defpis'd thy youth to manhood grew ;
 In manhood poor, a man difdain'd.

In perils oft, in painful toils and grief [a],
 Thy days were fpent—to blefs mankind ;
To give the wounded heart divine relief,
 And freedom to the captive mind.

To call the wand'ring in the darkfome road
 Of ignorance, and fin, and death ;
To charm them back to virtue, peace, and God,
 Employ'd the moments of thy breath [b].

———————————

[a] Ifaiah LIII. 3.   Luke IV. 28, 29.   Matt. XII. 14.
Mark III. 20, 21.   [b] Luke IV. 18, 19, 21.

At

At length, to finifh great redemption's plan,
  In duty to his father's will;
Extended on a crofs the wondrous man
  Expires—his mercy to fulfill [a].

Loud anthems hail'd thee to thy father's throne.,
  Virtue is thy imperial care.
Let the whole earth thy golden fcepter own,
  Let the whole earth its bleffings fhare.

❀❀❀❀❀❀❀❀❀❀❀❀❀❀❀❀❀❀❀❀❀❀

XVI.

JESUS CHRIST THE PHYSICIAN
OF SINNERS.

DIVINE Phyfician of the morbid [b] mind [c],
  Jefus; thy pow'rful fkill,
    For every moral ill,
  A fovereign remedy can find.

---

[a] Luke xxiv. 25—27.   1 Corinth. i. 3.   Ephef. i. 7.
Heb. x. 5, 7, 10.   [b] Difeafed.   [c] Matt. ix. 12, 13.

To

To reaſon, darken'd and infirm with ſin,
   Thou viſion canſt reſtore ᵃ,
   With ſtrength unknown before ;
And a new world in man begin ᵇ.

'Tis thy prerogative the ſoul to move ;
   The hard and ſtubborn heart
   Yields to thy ſoft'ning art,
Melts into grief, and glows with love.

The will in bondage, and to vice inur'd,
   Redeem'd, O Lord, by thee,
   Exults in liberty,
To righteouſneſs and God ſecur'd ᶜ.

The moſt unruly paſſions thou canſt tame,
   The fouleſt thou canſt clean,
   The gloomy make ſerene,
And change a tyger to a lamb.

ᵃ 1 Cor. 1. 30.   ᵇ Eph. 11. 10.
ᶜ John viii. 34, 36. Rom. vi. 18, 22.

O beau-

O beauteous work, benevolent, and great !
  With dignity of thought
  And generous paſſions fraught,
 And the ſweet peace of virtue's ſtate.

In virtue thy unrivall'd kingdom ſtands [a] ;
  Virtue thy conqueſts ſpreads,
  Thy hand the virtuous leads,
 All virtue's laws are thy commands.

His praiſe ſing aloud, ye children of day,
  Sing aloud his high name,
  And his glory proclaim,
 Who cloaths you in virtue's array [b].

To Calv'ry's martyr all glory be giv'n,
  Who will waſh us from ſtain [c],
  That with him we may reign [d],
 And walk in white raiment in heav'n [e].

---

[a] Pſalm xlv. 3, 4, 7. Rom. xiv. 17. [b] Rev. iii. 18.
[c] Joh. xiii. 8. Epheſ. v. 26, 27. Rev. i. 5, 6.
[d] Luke xxii. 29. 2 Tim. ii. 12. Rev. iii. 21.
[e] 2 Eſdras ii. 39, 40. Rev. iii. 4, 5. iv. 4. xix. 8.

XVII.

PRAISE TO GOD BY ALL MANKIND.

O Come, all ye fons of Adam ; and raife
  A fong unto God [a].   How lovely is praife [b].
Serve him, who reigns in his glory above,
And fills the wide earth with tokens of love.

His breath is your life, your reafon a ray
Effus'd from his light to guide all your way.
Your ficknefs he heals, your wants he fupplies, .
And wipes away tears from the penitent's eyes.

Dafh down your falfe gods of filver and gold,
Him worfhip who made earth and heav'n of old:
His fon, his falvation thankful receive,
Your follies confefs, obey him, and live.

---

[a] Pfalm cxvii. i.   Rom. xv. ii.
[b] Pfalm cxlvii. i.

O Father

O Father of men, in mercy command
Thy gofpel to fhine on all human land :
That far as the fun diffufes his beam,
Praife may afcend in Meffiah's great name [a].

XVIII.

THE SCRIPTURES [b].

TRUTH with her golden beam
    Infcribes th' immortal line:
Goodnefs and equity, fupreme,
    Through the bleft volume fhine.

In elocution plain
    Thefe heav'nly pages teach ;
And yet, their majefty of ftrain
    What mortal pen can reach ?

---

[a] Pfalm cxiii. 3. Pfalm ii. 8. Matt. vi. 10. Rom.
xv. 9, 10.   [b] See Pfalm xix, 7—11.

D

Here

Here precepts, old and new,
By God's own fignet bind :
With pow'rful wifdom thefe endue
The weak, but humble, mind.

Here promifes are fown,
Which holy ftrength infufe,
When dangers throng; or forrow's groan
Pleads for fupporting views.

O laws ! whofe vigour rends
The felf-accufing breaft :
Whofe vigour to the upright fends
Sweet felf-poffeffion's reft.

O promifes, whofe force
Is from all changes fecure !
Long as their everlafting fource,
Your bleffings fhall endure.

Hence warn'd, my fins I fee ;
Againft my fins I guard :
Hence aided, from perdition flee
To heav'n's immenfe reward.

Ye

Ye rich men, roll in gold ;
Ye epicures, in wine :
Your portion in contempt I hold ;
Thy word, O God, be mine [c].

XIX.

THE CHRISTIAN CHURCH.

JESUS with groans and blood redeem'd
    A people, to be ſtyl'd his own [d];
By virgin chaſtity of mind,
    And unpolluted manners known [e].

Illuſtrious unity of ſouls [f] !
    All the bright offspring of the day [g];
Like their eternal parent pure,
    Led and enliven'd by his ray [h].

---

[c] Pſalm cxix. 97, 103, 127.   [d] Acts xx. 28.
[e] Titus ii. 14.   [f] John xvii. 21.
[g] Luke xvi. 8. Joh. xii. 36. 1 Theſſ. v. 5.
[h] Matt. v. 48. Rom. viii. 15, 16. 1 Pet. i. 15, 23.
1 Joh. iii. 9, 10. Rom. viii. 14.

         Here

Here the great Father dwells, fupreme,
 And here his great vicegerent fon:
While life and blifs, from both deriv'd,
 Through the rejoicing houfhold run [i].

Sweet fellowfhip of peace and joy,
 'Tween man below and God above!
Delightful tie of man to man,
 By the ftrong pow'r of chriftian love [k]!

O bleft Community! who hold
 Titles divine, immortal claims [l]:
Heav'n's everlafting roll records,
 In letter'd gold, your worthy names [m].

The morn, the promis'd morn fhall beam,
 When your exalted faviour-king
Shall purge you from all finful fpot [n],
 And to his Father's prefence bring.

---

[i] John XIV. 20, 21, 23. 1 John I. 3.
[k] John XIII. 34, 35. John XVII. 23. Ephef. IV. 3.
[l] 1 Pet. I. 2—4. II. 4, 9.   [m] Luke x. 20, Rev.
XIII. 8.   [n] Ephef. v. 27, Jude 24, 25.

XX.

CHRISTIAN MINISTERS.

WELCOME, ye meſſengers of peace,
Ye ſervants of our mighty Lord:
May your juſt honours ne'er decreaſe,
Who labour to diſpenſe his word [o].

Ye leaders of the churches, ſtand;
Publiſh the ſtory of his love:
With his commiſſion in your hand,
Argue [p], exhort, conſole, reprove [q].

By your own lives exalt his laws,
His promiſe by your faith commend.
The glory of a Saviour's cauſe,
With his own gentle zeal defend [r].

---

[o] 1 Tim. v. 17. [p] Acts xvii. 2, 3. xxiv. 25. [q] 2 Tim. iii. 16, 17. iv. 2. 1 Theſſ. ii. 11. Iſaiah xl. 1. [r] 1 Tim. iv. 12.

Jefus, we yield a docile ear ;
   Such heralds of thy will and grace
With due fubmiffion we revere,
   With warm affection we embrace [s].

Profper, in all their anxious toil,
   Thefe faithful guardians of thy fheep [t] :
And from devouring hate and broil,
   Thy confecrated mountain keep [u].

****

XXI.

WISDOM's EXPOSTULATION
WITH SINNERS.

'TIS Wifdom's earneft cry ;
   Wifdom, the voice of God,
To young and old, the low and high,
   Utters his will abroad [w].

---

[s] Heb. xiii. 17.   [t] John xxi. 15, 16.
[u] Ifaiah xi. 9. lxv. 25.   [w] Prov. i. 20—22.

Within

Within the human breaſt,
Her ſtrong monitions plead.
She thunders her divine proteſt,
    Againſt th' unrighteous deed.

Within the holy place
She calls, with open arms ;
" How long ye fools will you embrace
    " Folly's deceiving charms [x].

    " The race of man I love [y],
    " In mercy I chaſtiſe,
" Severely faithful I reprove ;
    " Hear, mortals, and be wiſe [z].

    " My houſe, a royal pile [a],
    " Invites you through its gate.
" O leave the wilds of ſin and guile,
    " And enter ; ere too late.

---

[x] Prov. VIII. 1—5.　　[y] Prov. VIII. 31.
[z] Prov. VIII. 32, 33.　　[a] Prov. IX. 1—5.

　　　　　　" My

" My joys, unfenfual, tafte ;
" Come, drink of Wifdom's wine:
" No forrow poifons my repaft,
  " The banquet is divine.

" Honour and peace, with me,
" And life immortal dwell.
" Your ways of woe and infamy
  " Take hold of death and hell [b].

XXII.

WISDOM's THREATNING.

WISDOM exalts her voice again,
    I tremble at her awful ftrain :
With look fevere, and anger's tone,
She makes divine refentment known :
" Sinners, attend once more ; aftonifh'd hear
" The threatning I denounce ; its vengeance fear.

---

[b] Prov. viii. 18—21, 36. ix. 18. ii. 18, 19.

" Oft

" Oft I have publifh'd God's command,

" Oft I have wav'd my pleading hand,

" My eloquence I oft have try'd,

" And mercy's every means apply'd.

" But, unregarding, from my voice you turn'd,

" Scoff'd at my counfels, and my promife fpurn'd ᶜ.

" I too will fcoff, at your diftrefs

" When mazing fears your fouls opprefs :

" Scorn for your fcorn I will repay,

" In evil's defolating day ;

" When the black ftorm, long fwelling o'er your

  " heads,

" Impetuous burfts, and fwift deftruction fpreads.

" By ficknefs in her chain confin'd,

" Raving in agony of mind,

" While death ftands levelling his dart,

" Eager to bathe it in your heart ;

" To me, for refuge, you in vain fhall fly,

" Me importune with unavailing cry.

ᶜ Prov. 1. 20, 24—32.

" Your

" Your deeds of fin, and wit profane,
" Then bitterly bewail'd in vain,
" Inflam'd with glowing guilt fhall rife,
" And flafh my terrors in your eyes.
" Wrath in full meafure by yourfelves prepar'd,
" Obdurate finners, fhall your crimes reward."

✿✿✿✿✿✿✿✿✿✿✿✿✿✿✿✿✿✿✿✿✿

XXIII.

DELAY.

HASTEN, finners, to be wife [d];
    Stay not for the morrow's fun.
Longer wifdom you defpife,
    Harder is fhe to be won [e].

Haften, mercy to implore;
    Stay not for the morrow's fun :
Left thy feafon fhould be o'er,
    Ere this ev'ning's ftage be run.

---

[d] Pfalm cxix. 59, 60.   [e] Heb. iii. 13, 15.

Haſten, ſinner, to return ;
  Stay not for the morrow's ſun :
Leſt thy lamp ſhould fail to burn,
  Ere ſalvation's work is done [f].

Haſten, ſinner, to be bleſt ;
  Stay not for the morrow's ſun :
Leſt perdition thee arreſt,
  Ere the morrow is begun [g].

XXIV.

THE PENITENT.

YOUR flowing urns, ye fountains, lend [h],
  To fill theſe failing eyes ;
While mourning in the duſt I bend,
  Till mercy bid me riſe.

---

[f] Eccleſ. ix. 10.   [g] 2 Corinth. vi. 2.
[h] Jer. ix. 1.

Yes,

Yes, I have known, from childhood known,
   My God, thy holy will [i] :
Too negligent, I bluſhing own,
   Thy orders to fulfill.

Thy friendly voice, without, within,
   In cleareſt warnings ſpake :
" There winds the way of death and ſin,
   " The path of glory take."

Unheeding what thy voice advis'd,
   I went perverſely wrong ;
The caution and the hope deſpis'd,
   And madly ruſh'd along [k].

Sometimes I paus'd, and ſighing ſaid ;
   I will theſe ways forſake.
Soon, by ſome headſtrong luſt o'erſway'd,
   The feeble vow I brake.

---

[i] 2 Tim. iii. 15.   [k] Prov. i. 29, 30.

Ah !

Ah ! whither has my folly rov'd ?
   Loft on perdition's ground,
From thy ftill waters far remov'd,
   What pafture have I found [1] ?

Wand'ring for reft, where reft is none,
   By guilt and fear purfu'd ;
Idle, employ'd, in crowds, alone,
   Sad images I view'd [m].

Was this the great and good defign,
   For which I faw the day ?
Was reafon giv'n, that beam divine [n],
   Thus to be flung away ?

Ingrate thy bleffings I mifus'd,
   O thou long-fuff'ring Lord.
Thy law contemn'd and grace abus'd
   Demand thy damning word.

---

[1] Pfalm xxiii. 2.   [m] Ifaiah lvii. 20, 21.
[n] Prov. xx. 27.   Pfalm li. 6.

I hear

I hear, I hear foft mercy cry
　　(Sounds which my foul revive).
" O wherefore, finners, will ye die ?
　　" Children, return, and live °."

Before his Father's throne I fee ᴾ
　　The Mediator ftand.
Lo, while he pleads, to Calvary
　　He points with fpeaking hand.

My God with a fmile his full pardon difplays,
　　Defpair fhall for ever my bofom depart.
My glory awake ᑫ, fing aloud his high praife,
　　Sweet hope has begun to enliven my heart.

————————

° Jer. ɪɪɪ. 12, 14.　Ezek. xvɪɪɪ. 30—32.
ᴾ Heb. vɪɪ. 25. ɪx. 24.
ᑫ Pfalm Lvɪɪ. 8, 9. cvɪɪɪ. 1.

XXV.

CHRISTIAN PRIVILEGES AND OBLIGATIONS.

D OST thou my worthlefs name record
    Free of thy holy city, Lord ʳ?
Am I, a finner, call'd to fhare
The precious privileges there?

Art thou, my king my father ftyl'd?
And I, thy fervant and thy child ˢ?
While more than half the human race
Are aliens from thy Zion's grace ᵗ.

Lo, wretched millions draw their breath
In lands of ignorance and death ᵘ.
But I enjoy my line of time,
Within thy gofpel's favourite clime.

ʳ Ephef ii. 19.   ˢ Ephef. i. 5.
ᵗ Ephef. ii. 12.   ᵘ Matt. iv. 16.

4   Pardon

Pardon aſſur'd and heav'n diſplay'd,
Baniſh my fears, my hope perſuade ͫ:
And precepts, plentiful and clear ˣ,
Through life my dang'rous voyage ſteer.

Shall I receive this grace in vain ʸ ?
Shall I my great vocation ſtain ᶻ ?
Away, ye works in darkneſs wrought ͣ;
Away, each mean and wanton thought.

My ſoul, I charge thee to excell
In thinking right and acting well.
Deep, deep, thy ſearching pow'rs engage,
Unbiaſs'd, in the heav'n-born page.

Heighten the force of good deſire,
To deeds of ſhining worth aſpire:
More firm in fortitude, deſpiſe
The world's ſeducing vanities.

ͫ Luke xxiv. 47.   ˣ Coloſſ. iv. 12.   Epheſ. v. 17.
Rom. xii. 2.   ʸ 2 Corinth. vi. 1:   ᶻ Epheſ. iv. 1.
ͣ Epheſ. v. 11.

Strong

Strong and more ſtrong, thy paſſions rule ;
Advancing ſtill in virtue's ſchool ;
Contending ſtill, with noble ſtrife,
To emulate thy Saviour's life [b].

XXVI.

NEED OF DIVINE ASSISTANCE.

TO fix the thought on things above,
 To give them pow'r the heart to move,
To hold futurity in view ;
What can a feeble mortal do ?

To warm the foul with love to God,
To tremble at his lifted rod,
To keep the will to conſcience true ;
What can a feeble mortal do ?

[b] 1 Pet. ii. 21.

E

To

To live by faith, to combat hell,
The world's temptations to repell,
And self-denial's path pursue ;
What can a feeble mortal do [c] ?

Lord, this stupendous work is thine ;
The sacrifice of praise be mine,
Oft as thy aids my force renew ;
What can a feeble mortal do ?

XXVII.

CHRISTIAN WARFARE.

THE captain of Jehovah's armies stands,
   Th' imperial banner is aloft display'd.
Flow to his ensign, all his valiant bands,
   And bravely fight beneath it's pow'rful shade [d].

---

[c] Pfalm LI. 10. CXIX. 18, 35—37, 66. John xv. 4, 5.
xvii. 15. Philip. iv. 13. 1 Pet. i. 5. v. 10. Jude 24.
  [d] Heb. ii. 10. 1 Tim. i. 18, 19. 1 Tim. vi. 12.
Tim. iii. 3.

Clad

Clad in celeſtial arms, of nobler frame
   Than thoſe ᵉ renown'd in the Mæonian ſong;
Ye heroes, panting for immortal fame,
   In great Immanuel's conqu'ring might be ſtrong.

Her ᶠ *zone Uprightneſs* round your loins ſhall caſt,
   The mind's unweary'd vigour to ſuſtain.
In *Virtue's cuiraſs* ſheath'd, meet, unaghaſt,
   The charms of pleaſure and the force of pain.

Sandal'd with *zeal* your active feet will tread
   The cragged mountain, and the rocky road;
When the bleſt goſpel ſummons you, to ſpread
   The healing odour of its truth abroad.

The fiery ſhafts of furious *luſts* defy,
   Dauntleſs oppoſe faith's adamantine *ſhield*.
Salvation's helmet to your head apply,
   For dangerous war in ſcepticiſm's field.

ᵉ The invulnerable arms of Achilles deſcribed by Homer in his Iliad.   ᶠ Epheſ. vɪ. 10—17.

     Th' ethereal

Th' ethereal *blade* ne'er loofen from your fide,
   The word of God, fo formidably keen :
This weapon your victorious chieftain try'd,
   In bold temptation's moft audacious fcene ᵍ.

Thus dreft in panoply ʰ divine, prepare
   For ftrenuous ftrife and perfevering toil.
Advance, with martial ftep and martial air,
   The foes of righteoufnefs and God to foil.

An amaranthine ⁱ crown of glory ᵏ waits,
   To dignify the faithful foldier's brows :
His labours o'er, high Salem opes her gates,
   And bow'rs of blifs invite him to repofe ᶦ.

ᵍ Matt. iv. 4, 7, 10.   ʰ *panoply*, a complete
fuit of armour.   ⁱ *amaranthine*, unfading.

   ᵏ 1 Pet. v. 4.   ᶦ Heb. iv. 1, 9—11. Rev. xiv.
13. XXII. 14.

XXVIII.

THE SAME SUBJECT IN A DIFFERENT METRE.

JESUS his banner has difplay'd,
 Hell threatens formidable war.
All o'er in heav'nly arms array'd,
 Unmov'd her haughty pow'rs I dare.

Truth, like a *belt*, fhall gird me round,
 And vigour in my foul fuftain.
With *Virtue*, as a breaft-plate, bound,
 Temptation's onfet I difdain.

Meeknefs fhall on my march attend,
 Meeknefs fhall rage and fpite defeat :
Not greaves of brafs can more defend,
 From cruel fpikes the foldier's feet.

Come, *Faith*, and bring thy temper'd *fhield*,
 This to the furious foe oppofe :
Vanquifh'd, with fhame he quits the field,
 In vain his fiery darts he throws.

Salva-

Salvation's hope my head ſhall ſhade,
　　A, helmet of celeſtial frame:
Thy word, O Lord, all-conqu'ring *blade*,
　　With terror on the foe ſhall flame.

XXIX.

B L E S S E D N E S S [m].

THRICE happy man! whoſe youthful feet
　　Touch not the path which ſinners beat:
Or *walk* not in the fatal way,
Where *unrepenting* ſinners ſtray
Till, oft alas! their impious tongue
Mimics the harden'd *ſcoffing* throng.

Thrice happy man! whoſe ſoul's deſire
To honour God is all on fire:

---

[m] See Pſalm 1.

Who

Who on his holy volume feeds,
Warm'd with the love of virtuous deeds;
Revolving fweetly, on his bed,
The leffons which by day he read.

Like a fair tree, with foliage green
Long by the garden currents feen;
Whofe lovely flow'rs in feafon blow,
And to a generous vintage grow,
He flourifhes; in worth of mind,
Heav'n-blefs'd, the joy of human kind.

Not fo the wicked in their place,
A vile unprofitable race:
Out of the living they are caft,
Like chaff before the rifing blaft,
And in fome future day fhall fall
Convicts, before the judge of all.

In that high day, the righteous Band
Exulting at his bar fhall ftand:
His fentence will their way approve,
And lift them to his feat above.
His fentence on the bad will frown,
And drive them to perdition down.

E 4

XXX.

BENEFIT OF EARLY PIETY.

COME, children, learn the heav'nly art,
    To make your growing years
All happy, and defend your heart
    From guilt, diftrefs, and fears.

Remember him who gave you breath [n],
    Remember him who dy'd
To fave you from eternal death :
    His precepts be your guide [o].

What ornaments a young man grace,
    In piety approv'd [p] !
How lovely virtue's blooming face !
    By God and man belov'd.

———————————

[n] Ecclef. xii. 1.   [o] Pfalm cxix. 9.
[p] Prov. iv. 7—9.

Virtue

Virtue in early youth begun
  The man with eafe purfues ?;
And when his mortal courfe is run,
  In heav'n his life renews.

O fquander not your nobleft time
  In vanity and fin :
Left death fhould pluck you in your prime,
  And hell fhould fnatch you in.

Fond parents, with religious care
  Your tender offspring train :
Warn them of every ambufh'd fnare,
  Sow, fow the pious grain.

Thus the great Father gives command ',
  Thus fpeaks a parent's love.
Know, judgment's awful day, at hand,
  Your faithfulnefs will prove.

? Prov. xxii. 6.   ' Eph. vi. 4.

XXXI.

THE VOW.

MY heart is fix'd, the firm decree
   Is ratify'd within my breast.
I vow my soul, O Lord, to thee ˢ,
   In thee alone I seek my rest ᵗ.

Adieu, ye vain desires, adieu ;
   Ye lusts of every name, farewell :
I bar all fellowship with you ᵘ,
   I mean no more to live for hell.

In dissipation's magic ground,
   In busy scenes of toil and care,
What pleasures or what gains are found,
   Which may with thine, O Lord, compare ʷ ?

ˢ Psalm cxix. 106. 2 Corinth. viii. 5.
ᵗ Psalm lxxiii. 25, 26. Jer. vi. 16.   ᵘ Ephes.
v. 11. Titus ii. 11, 12. ʷ Psalm iv. 6, 7. Prov.
iii. 17. Psalm xix. 11.

       Pleasures

Pleafures which yield no peace, I leave;
　　Wealth but a fpoil for death, I fpurn:
Hopes I embrace which ne'er deceive [x],
　　For wealth which never dies [y], I burn.

To faith's heroic war I rife,
　　Nor dread my ftrong and wily foes;
Safe in the arms thy word fupplies,
　　Led by the wifdom it beftows.

My heart is fix'd, the firm decree
　　Is ratify'd within my breaft.
I vow my foul, O Lord, to thee,
　　In thee alone I feek my reft.

———————————

[x] Rom. v. 5.　　　　[y] Luke xii. 33.

XXXII.

PRAYER.

OUR Father, thron'd above the fkies,
 To thee my empty hands I fpread.
Thy child of duft beneath thee lies,
 Who afks thy blefling on his head.

Let mercy all my fins difpell,
 As a dark cloud before the beam [*].
My foul from bondage and from hell,
 To liberty and life redeem.

With chearful hope and filial fear,
 In that auguft and precious name
By thee ordain'd, I now draw near;
 And would the promis'd blefling claim [a].

------

[*] Ifaiah XLIV. 22.
[a] Gal. iv. 6, 7. Heb. x. 19—22.

On thy good promifes I lean,
   Thy truth can never never fail [b];
Though ftedfaft earth and heav'n's great fcene
   Shall perifh [c], like an ev'ning tale.

Will not an earthly parent feel
   The cravings of his child in need !
Will he prefent a cake of fteel
   For bread, his hungry mouth to feed [d]?

Our heav'nly Father, how much more
   Will thy divine compaffions rife;
And open thy unbounded ftore,
   To fatisfy thy childrens cries ?

Yes, I will afk, and feek, and prefs,
   For gracious audience, to thy feat;
Still hoping, waiting, for fuccefs
   If perfevering to intreat [e].

---

[b] Pfalm cxix. 90. cxlvi. 6.   Heb. x. 23.   1 Pet.
1. 23.   2 Pet. 1. 2, 4.   [c] Heb. 1. 10—12.   2 Pet.
iii. 11—13.   [d] Matt. vii. 7—11.
   [e] Luke xviii. 1.   Job xxiii. 3.

For

For Jefus, in his faithful word,
    The patient fupplicant has blefs'd:
And all thy faints, with fweet accord,
    The prevalence of pray'r atteft.

XXXIII.

CONFESSION.

O GOD the holy and the juft,
    Look not with anger's flafhing eye,
Behold me proftrate in the duft,
    Hear a lamenting finner's figh.

My fins like ocean's fands abound,
    My fins are ftain'd with crimfon hue:
The'r burden finks me to the ground,
    To heav'n I dare not lift my view.

---

f Pfalm xxxviii. 4. xl. 12.

Above

Above the fowls that fwim in air,
 Above the beafts which graze below;
Reafon, thy noble gift, I fhare;
 By reafon taught, thy laws I know [g].

How bleft! if I to reafon's voice
 Had yielded an obeying ear:
Bleft! if thy will had been my choice,
 Thou my delight, and thou my fear [h].

But oh! the paffions in my frame,
 Inwrought by thee for wifeft end,
With blindfold violence o'ercame
 Reafon, and confcience reafon's friend [i].

In reafon's aid thy gofpel ftrove,
 I heeded not, but onward ran:
The ways of ruin were my love [k],
 O what a ftubborn thing is man!

---

[g] Job xxxv. 11. xxxii. 8. [h] Pfalm i. 1, &c.
[i] James i. 13, 14. [k] Prov. viii. 36.

Er,

Lord, I am worthy to receive
  The dreadful fentence, " Thou fhalt die ¹ :"
But ere the fatal ftroke thou give,
  Turn, turn thy face to Calvary.

❀❀❀❀❀❀❀❀❀❀❀❀❀❀❀❀❀❀❀❀❀❀

XXXIV.

PETITION
FOR DEVOTIONAL VIEWS.

HOW long, O Lord, and why,
    Wilt thou thy glories fhade ?
How long unheeded fhall my cry
    Thy gentle ear invade ᵐ ?

Whene'er my feeble thought
On heav'nly things would mufe ;
The vifions, to thy people brought ⁿ,
    Their charms to me refufe.

---

¹ Pfalm LI. 4. Ezek. XVII. 4.   ᵐ Pfalm XIII. 1.
XXII. 1, 2.   ⁿ Pfalm CXIX. 18, 66, 169, 171.
Ephef. 1. 17—20. Prov. II. 3—5.
                                              Wifdom

Wifdom and works of pow'r,
Which in thy gofpel fhine,
On me in wafte their fun-beams fhow'r.
O this blind foul of mine!

Thy miracles of love
To me no joy impart;
In me no tender paffion move.
O my unfeeling heart!

If I to Jefus turn,
Nail'd to the cruel tree;
With no feraphic love I burn,
Although he dy'd for me.

Whene'er my fins I call
Before ftern judgment's eye;
Scarce a bewailing tear will fall,
I fcarce can heave a figh.

Thy promifes I lay
Clofe to my aking breaft:
Fain would I hope, hope flees away—
My anguifh finds no reft.

F   In

In darknefs muft I go,
    An alien ftill from thee ?
Ah ! never fhall my bofom know
    The glow of piety ?

And muft I then defpair ?
    Is there no laft refource ?
Though nature fails, Ah yet—elfewhere
    Lives no affifting force ?

Who, who, is he ; that ftands
    Before thy gracious throne ?
That lifts his interceding hands,
    When humble finners groan ° ?

To whom has thy decree
    Wifdom for finners giv'n ᴾ ?
Will not his grace indulge to me,
    Some of that beam of heav'n ?

° Heb. ɪv. 14—16. vɪɪ. 24, 25.
ᴾ 1 Corinth. ɪ. 30.

Unclofe,

Unclofe, unclofe thefe eyes,
Infufe the vifual ray :
Before me bid thy glories rife,
With foul-reviving day.

XXXV.

SUSPENSION OF DIVINE INFLUENCES.

O the diftracting fears [q],
Which rent my heart in twain;
The fighs, and groans, and burfting tears
Of forrow's fharpeft pain ;

When firft my God refrain'd
His mercy to purfue ;
And, ere his work perfection gain'd,
His energy withdrew.

---

[q] Pfalm LVIII. 13—15.

A deep

A deep and deadly gloom
O'er mental vifion fweeps :
Benumbing cold, O fearful doom !
O'er mental feelings creeps.

I threw me at his feet,
In bitternefs of heart :
My piercing cries affail'd his feat;
Will, will my God depart ?

Is it thy way to leave
A turning finner fo [r] ?
Thy joy a broken heart to grieve [s],
And quench the fmoking tow [t] ?

Ah ! no—'tis thy delight
To hear confeffion's breath [u] :
To fet the ftraying footftep right [w],
And fave a foul from death [x].

---

[r] Pfalm IX. 10.   [s] Pfalm LI. 17.
[t] Ifaiah XLII. 3.   [u] Pfalm XXXII. 5.
[w] Pfalm XXIII. 3. CXIX. 176.
[x] Ezek. XXXIII. 11.

O plen-

O plentiful in love ʸ,
O ready to forgive ᶻ,
Let fighs and tears thy bowels move ᵃ :
Say to a finner, " live."

XXXVI.

MOURNING AFTER GOD.

WHAT new offence, what unknown deed
      Has driv'n my God away ᵇ ?
Why is it that in vain I plead ?
    Oh ! why this long delay ?

Thoughts after thoughts all day enfue,
    In melancholy train.
Sorrow, I lay me down with you,
    With you I rife again ᶜ.

ʸ Pfalm cɪɪɪ. 3, 8, 9.   ᶻ Pfalm Lxxxvɪ. 5.
ᵃ Pfalm vɪ. 6. xxxɪx. 12. xxxɪ. 10.
ᵇ Job xxxɪv. 32. Ifaiah Lɪx. 2.   ᶜ Pfalm xɪɪɪ. 1, 2.
xxxvɪɪɪ. 4, 6.
            F 3   The

The holy leaves, I fighing faid,
  Will eafe my preffing woe:
Their light fhall o'er my foul be fpread,
  Their comforts in me flow [d].

Eager the holy leaves I turn,
  I ftrain attention's pow'rs.
Alas ! in darknefs ftill I mourn,
  Still comfortlefs my hours.

Hope whifpers, " in his holy place
  Thou fhalt the bleffing find [e]."
Hope blufhes, for he hides his face;
  And grief o'erwhelms my mind.

Yet I will feek him till I die;
  Who always fought in vain [f] ?
His heart is kind, his pow'r is nigh,
  And pray'r his ear will gain [g].

---

[d] Pfalm cxix. 50, 130.   [e] Pfalm lxiii. 2.
lxv. 4.   [f] Pfalm ix. 10. xxvii. 14. Ifaiah xlv. 19.
[g] Pfalm lxv. 2.

XXXVII.

THE RESOLUTION.

HOW long ere weeping Elegy
   Bid me adieu, and hafte away ?
How long, ere fweet Euphrofyne [h]
   To me her fparkling charms difplay ?

Not while my God in frowns conceals [i],
   The beauties of his fmiling face ;
Not till my longing bofom feels,
   The extafies of pard'ning grace.

Not till, in pow'r immortal ftrong,
   I burft the iron yoke of fin ;
Till, number'd with the ranfom'd throng,
   Their heav'n within my foul begin.

---

[h] Joy.   [i] Pfalm LXXVII. 2—4.

F 4   Come,

Come, hour long fought; on rapid wing
Bear thy fweet inmate, holy Mirth.
Then, then my founding voice fhall fing,
The wonders of celeftial birth.

XXXVIII.

TRANSIENT GOODNESS.

WHERE, O my foul, O where
Thy image fhall I view ?
In the light cloud which melts in air,
Or in the early dew [k].

This hour, with flowing tears
My follies I bewail:
The next, my heart a wafte appears,
Where all the fountains fail.

---

[k] Hof, vi. 4.

Now,

Now, as the wax in flame
Diffolves, and loves the feal;
The tend'reft touch of grief and fhame
Alternately I feel.

To day, her glimmering light
Hope kindles in my breaft:
The morrow, with defpair's black night,
Has all my foul oppreft.

O my unftedfaft mind,
Toft between good and ill!
With fteady courfe the brutal kind
Their Maker's law fulfill.

O miferable ftate,
Of hope by fear fubdu'd!
On thee, O Lord, for help I wait;
Fix, fix my foul in good [1].

---

[1] James i. 8. 1 Pet. v. 10.

XXXIX.

DEJECTION.

AH! never, never fhall I tafte the joy
   Which to thy children, Lord, belongs [m]?
Never one favour'd pray'r my tongue employ,
   In melody of Zion's fongs!

Thou fulgent lamp, in whofe all-cheering beams
   The living clans of earth rejoice;
While fields, and hills, and woods, and fparkling
     ftreams
   Eccho to joy's exulting voice;.

To me, alas! the light of morning gay,
   Like gloom of midnight is difplay'd:
To me thy noontide and thy weftern ray,
   Is all but melancholy fhade.

---

[m] Pfalm cvi. 4, 5.

A weight

A weight of woe lies heavy on my heart,
   Whole days and tedious months I mourn ;
Since the fad hour I felt my God depart :
   Ah ! never will my God return [n] ?

Life's fweet amufements all in vain engage,
   To yield my troubled foul relief :
Nor friendly converfe, nor the ftory'd page,
   Can charm to peace my reftlefs grief.

Lord, yield one gracious look : one fmile of thine
   Shall caufe my ravifh'd heart to bound ;
More than the feafon of o'erflowing wine,
   When the glad vintage-fhouts refound [o].

---

[n] Pfalm LXXVII, 7—9.   [o] Pfalm IV. 6, 7.

XL.

ADDRESS TO JESUS CHRIST.

IMMANUEL, Saviour, meek and mild,
　　To thee I pour my moan.
Behold a wretch, with fin defil'd,
　　Who looks to thee alone P.

O Prince of life, all pow'r is thine
　　To pardon and fubdue q :
My pardon, in thy mercy, fign,
　　My foul to God renew.

Give to thy holy angels joy r,
　　Their hallelujahs fire:
Let thy rich grace to me employ,
　　Afrefh, each golden Lyre.

———————

P John III. 14. compared with Numb. xxi. 9.   Acts
IV. 12. Eph. I. 12. Jude 20, 21.
q Acts III. 15. v. 31.   Matt. IX. 6. xxviii. 19.
r Luke xv. 7.

Me

Me a new captive in thy train,
　　And in thy book ' enroll'd ;
Me a new glory of thy reign,
　　Let thy great Sire behold.

O thou, who in thy mortal days
　　Didſt with the ſighing ſigh ;
Shall not my tears thy pity raiſe,
　　Though now thou art ſo high ?

Who ever humbly kneel'd in vain,
　　Before thy gracious ſeat ?
O do not my warm ſuit diſdain,
　　Nor puſh me from thy feet ' !

' Luke x. 20.　Revel. xxi. 27.
' Matt. xi. 28.　John vi. 37.

XLI.

C O M P L A I N T.

HOW ſtrange are his myſterious ways !
    What numbers can his wonders tell ?
My ſoul in vain the ſearch eſſays,
    'Tis high as heav'n, 'tis deep as hell ᵘ.

Why did his hand, unſought by me,
    Stop me in folly's fatal race ?
Why teach my trembling ſoul, to flee
    To Jeſus for his healing grace.

Why did he melt my heart, with grief
    My treſpaſs in his ear to own ?
Then ſudden check ſweet hope's relief ?
    And leave me hard again as ſtone ?

———————————————

ᵘ Job xi. 7—9. ix. 10.

Ah !

Ah ! did he ever thus forfake
  The blind, who mourn'd for faving light?
Why fuffer me one glance to take ?
  Then fnatch the vifion from my fight ?

Was he, whofe half-enlighten'd eye
 · Saw men appear as walking trees ᵂ,
Left in the bitter mifery
  Of a bewail'd half-cur'd difeafe ?

Ceafe, mortal ceafe, in plaintive ftrain,
  Thy Maker's counfels to implead.
Wifdom and mercy guide his reign,
  In righteoufnefs his acts proceed ˣ.

How ftrange are his myfterious ways !
  What numbers can his wonders tell ?
My toil in vain the fearch effays,
  'Tis high as heav'n, 'tis deep as hell.

ᵂ Mark VIII. 24.   ˣ Pfalm CXLV. 17. Jer. IX. 24.

7

XLII.

THANKSGIVING.

YES—it was Thou, whofe gracious care
   Educ'd me from the womb,
Sent me to drink thy healthful air,
   And nurs'd my tender bloom ʸ.

Thy gentle hand my feet upheld,
   In childhood's flippery way :
Ere yet my tongue thy name had fpell'd,
   Thy name was all my ftay ᶻ.

My ripening years were ftill purfu'd
   With mercies from above :
Thy bounty raiment gave, and food,
   And loaded me with love ᵃ.

ʸ Pfalm xxII. 9, 10.   ᶻ Pfalm LXXI. 6.
ᵃ Job x. 12. Pfalm cIII. 2—5. cxxxIX. 17, 18.

When

If trouble's heavy arm was near,
   Thy pity felt my figh;
Knew all my forrow, all my fear,
   And brought falvation nigh [b].

When I behold yon azure fpace
   Spangled with ftars, and fee
Th'imperial moon's refulgent face;
   Wond'ring, I think on thee.

Lord, what is man, that man fhould gain
   Thy condefcending view?
That e'er thy majefty fhould deign,
   Such favour to renew [c]?

And what am I, leaft worthy I
   Of all who creep below,
That thou wilt pafs my follies by,
   And fo much goodnefs fhow [d]?

---

[b] Pfalm xxxi. 7. xxxiv. 6.   [c] Pfalm viii. 3, 4.

[d] Gen. xxxii. 10.

O fummon

O fummon thy whole ftrength, my foul,
　　To blefs thy God alone.
O memory, all his boons enroll;
　　I charge thee, lofe not one ᵉ.

❀❀❀❀❀❀❀❀❀❀❀❀❀❀❀❀❀❀❀❀

XLIII.

PRAYER

OF THE AFFLICTED YOUTH.

MY Sovereign, to thy throne
　　With awful hope I prefs.
Humble thyfelf to hear the groan
　　Of indigent diftrefs.

Thy royal Prieft appears
　　Before thee with his blood ᶠ:
Through him I offer thefe my tears ᵍ,
　　And caft my care on God ʰ.

ᵉ Pfalm cⅢ. 1, 2.　　　ᶠ Heb. vⅡ. 15—17.
ᵍ John xvⅠ. 23, 24.　Heb. Ⅸ. 24.　　ʰ Pfalm Lv. 22.

　　　　　　　　　　　　　Mʃ

My youth, bow'd down with pain,
Mourns its decaying bloom.
Lord, clothe thefe bones with flefh again;
O fpare me from the tomb [1].

Without one murm'ring word,
Thy chaft'ning I receive [k];
But afk, fubmiffive, gracious Lord,
A merciful reprieve.

Day following day, my pray'r
Has wreftled with thy grace.
Let not confufion be the fhare,
Of them who feek thy face [1].

Was e'er thy bounteous mind
Unwilling to beftow [m]?
E'er to a finner's fighs unkind,
Or in forgiving flow [n]?

---

[1] Pfalm xxxix. 13. cii. 24. Job xxxiii. 25.
[k] Pfalm xxxix. 9. Heb. xii. 5, 6. [1] Pfalm xxv. 3.
[m] James i. 5. [n] Pfalm lxxvi. 5. ciii. 8, 9.

Needy

Needy and poor, as now,
I once thy aid implor'd :
Thy pity heard affliction's vow,
Thy pow'r my health reftor'd.

My fupplicating voice
Unweary'd I will raife :
Say to thy fervant's foul, " rejoice ;"
And fill my tongue with praife [n].

XLIV.

SOLILOQUY.

DEEP, deep into thyfelf, my foul defcend;
   God calls aloud, with rev'rent ear attend.
Strikes he in vain ? unmeaning was the blow [o] ?
Sudden it fell, and menac'd death and woe ;
Death to a life in which my life is bound,
Woe, woe to me, and never-healing wound :

---

[n] Pfalm XLII. 11.   [o] The fmall-pox.

She

She lives! she lives! But Ah! is Heav'n appeas'd?
Or, next, am I the victim to be seiz'd?
Does old offence to his remembrance rise ^p,
And bid the tear repentant fill my eyes?
My heart relents, my broken spirit mourns,
To thee, O Lord, my broken spirit turns.
Forgiving God, cast, cast my sins away,
Far as the rising from the setting day ^q.
Spare me, O Lord, my tender offspring spare,
Let not the child the father's burden bear ^r.
Avert this direful pest ^s. O heal my son,
Bid life's warm fluid through its channels run;
With healthful vigour bid the lungs inhale ^t,
Eas'd of their load, thy vivifying gale.
With balmy hope erect his drooping mind,
With patience arm, and give the will resign'd.
Keep his youth pure, to shining virtue raise,
And crown that virtue with celestial praise.

---

^p Psalm xxv. 6.   ^q Psalm ciii. 12.
^r Jer. xxxi. 29. Ezek. xviii. 2—4.
^s The small-pox.   ^t Asthma.

G 3

XLV.

T H O U G H T S
ON A PARTICULAR MERCY.

HAIL, dear abode; my irkſome exile ' ends.
 Farewel diſquietude and ſleepleſs care :
Come, Peace, with thy beatitudes: my friends,
 Aſſiſt our triumph, and the feſtal ſhare.

Long has diſeaſe, Heav'n's miniſter, poſſeſs'd
 This mourning manſion with her pois'nous train,
Indulgent Pow'r, forbid that evil gueſt
 To trouble theſe deliver'd walls again.

Here may the pray'r, from undiſſembling tongue,
 Sound into heav'n ; the fervid praiſe aſcend,
Diurnal incenſe; and a gracious throng -
 Of bleſſings o'er this favour'd roof impend.

' On account of the ſmall-pox.

Hail

Hail fweet retirement, where the Mufe once more
  Shall in calm filence prune her ruffled wing;
With modern Bards and ancient wifdom foar,
  And mortal themes and themes immortal fing.

All hail ! thou nobleft gift which Heav'n beftow'd
  On me unworthy, worthy to have loft ;
Dear fellow pilgrim on this earthly road,
  'The vale of grief, to the celeftial coaft.

Victorious in affliction's field, thy mind
  Shines with new luftre, in new graces dreft ;
Patience and faith thy head with garlands bind,
  And God approves, and heav'n is in thy breaft.

G 4

XLVI.

THE YOUTH's
THANKSGIVING ODE.

ᵘ TO Jehovah, thou my foul
  Give the tributary glory:
Mem'ry, all his love enroll,
 Crowded is the boundlefs ftory,

All thy maladies he heals,
 All thy trefpaffes forgiving:
Death's commiffion he repeals,
 He reftores thee to the living.

Healthful viands he beftows,
 With new youth thy flefh recruiting;
As an eagle's plumage grows,
 With new vigour from their fhooting.

ᵘ See Pfalm cⅢ.

6

With

With his love thy days are crown'd,
  Thy requests are always near him:
High as heav'n above the ground,
  Is that love to them who fear him.

They who fear him daily learn,
  For their frailties his compaſſion :
So a father's mercies yearn,
  To his children in tranſgreſſion.

Well he knows their fleſhly frame
  Of weak elements compounded:
Nor is harſh their ſouls to blame,
  With infirmities furrounded.

What is man ? a feeble flow'r
  For a feaſon ſweetly blooming ;
Soon the rugged eaſt wind's pow'r
  All its tender life conſuming.

In the evening tall and fair,
  Gone for ever in the morning ;
Seen no more, forgotten where
  Once it ſtood the field adorning.

XLVII.

PAIN.

Y E tedious hours of pain,
  When will ye roll away?
Ah! when fhall I enjoy, again,
The well man's eafy day?

* *Lives*, then, the child of fin,
  Yet breathes impatient fighs?
Know, from thyfelf thy woes begin,
From guilt thy forrows rife.

Is not thy Maker love ˣ?
 Is not his anger flow ʸ?
Do not our griefs his pity move?
Can he enjoy our woe ᶻ?

---

* Lament. iii. 39.   ˣ 1 John iv. 16.
ʸ Nehem. ix. 17.   ᶻ Lament. iii. 32, 33.

Compaf-

Compaſſionate, he ſees
His human offspring ſtray;
And oft commiſſions ſharp diſeaſe
Our wild career to ſtay [a].

Soon as contrition's eye
Is full, with humble tear;
He bids all-healing mercy fly,
The fainting heart to cheer [b].

O the reviving grace
His promiſes diſtill!
Almighty anodyne! they chaſe
The pain from every ill [c].

Learn, learn, my ſoul, to wait,
Till thy releaſe is giv'n.
Bleſs him, who made a ſuff'ring ſtate
The pupillage for heav'n.

---

[a] Job xxxiii. 19. Heb. xii. 10. [b] Job xxiii.
27, 28. [c] Pſalm cxix. 50.

XLVIII.

RECOVERY.

HOW lively the pleasure succeeding to pain!
   When disease says " adieu;" and health comes
      again,
New braces the limbs, new enlightens the eyes,
And the faint-beating heart with spirits supplies.

The mariner, when his rough voyage is o'er,
Talks over his perils, exulting on shore:
The wind in his canvas still thund'ring he hears,
The high foaming billows still clash in his ears.

So let me revolve the long wearisome night,
Of sorrow's lone room and sorrow's sharp fight;
The storms of fierce pain, hot fever's strong thirst,
And the bubble of life just ready to burst.

As a bird manumis'd essays his rude wings,
Expatiates in air, and a loud carol sings;
Enlarging my steps, o'er the fields I will rove,
And join the full choir that enlivens the 'grove.

                                        Bright

Bright fun, how delightfome to feel thy warm ray!
Your ftreams, ye gay meadows, how fweet to furvey!
Delicious perfume floats along in the gale,
Frefh fpirits and force with each guft I inhale.

Now my friends I embrace, their converfe enjoy,
My ftation's great duties my time now employ.
The mind its accuftom'd exertions difplays,
The body, recruited for labour, obeys.

All praife to my God, who in mercy repriev'd
A finner from death, and his anguifh reliev'd:
To fave me from ruin he chaften'd my faults,
And to care of my foul awaken'd my thoughts.

Who, unwilling to bruife a reptile of duft,
His ftroke long delays, though the ftripe would be
        juft:
At laft when he fmites (for to anger he's flow)
With a father's foft hand he tempers the blow d.

By him I revive, with my juvenile bloom;
And my pow'rs of thinking new vigour refume.
To him while I breathe, devout homage I'll bring,
My portion, my hope, and my almighty king.

————————————

d Prov. iii. 11, 12.

XLIX.

THE AGED MINISTER

FALLING DOWN IN A FAINTING FIT IN THE
PLACE AND TIME OF PUBLIC WORSHIP.

WHAT a fudden paufe is here !
   Silence ftops the pray'r afcending—
Pannic fmites attention's ear,
   Order in confufion blending.

Son of wifdom, faint, awake
   From the trance of fainting nature.
Cloud on reafon's organ, break ;
   Gracious God, the darknefs fcatter.

Does the king of fears advance,
   His black hoft of pains difplaying?
Does he fhake his murd'ring lance.?
   Empty terrors, undifmaying.

Upwards

Upwards turn thy ravish'd eyes,
  See the world of glory moving,
From their thrones the just arise;
  See thy God with smiles approving.

On the verge of heav'n they stand,
  Thy expected flight beholding:
See the crown in Jesus' hand,
  See the gate of pearl unfolding.

From his trance the faint awakes,
  Heav'n consenting to restore him,
From our lips the triumph breaks;
  Late, O late, may we deplore him.

L.

THE AGED MINISTER

OBLIGED BY ILL HEALTH TO LAY DOWN HIS OFFICE.

HOW pleafant roll'd the days !
  When, hanging o'er my head;
Thy lamp, O Lord, its vivid rays
  Around my footfteps fpread ᵉ :

When all my vigorous pow'rs
  Sent all their ftrength abroad;
And fill'd up all my active hours
  With fervice of my God :

When crowds about me hung,
  Impatient for the theme
Divine, fweet-flowing from my tongue;
  And drank falvation's ftream.

ᵉ Job xxix. 3.

Now

Now darkneſs caſts her veil
  All o'er my troubled ſky.
Thy hand afflicting I bewail ;
  Thy healing hand apply.

Shall a ſlack'd thread of clay
  Untune the reas'ning mind ?
Shall memory mourn her ſtores, a prey
  To malady reſign'd ?

God of my frame, I bow
  My reaſon to thy will :
And only breathe this humble vow,
  May I thy work fulfill [f].

---

[f] 2 Tim. IV. 5.

H

LI.

TRUST IN THE PROMISE OF PARDON.

WHEREFORE this flownefs to believe
　　The God who cannot lie?
How can my feeble thoughts conceive
　　Of clemency fo high?

Alas, my fins! their fum fo great,
　　And of fo foul a die!
Will he forgive th' enormous debt?
　　O clemency, fo high!

His thoughts of mercy are immenfe;
　　Above our thoughts they fly,
ɛ Lofty as heav'n above our fenfe.
　　O clemency, fo high!

ɛ Ifaiah ʟv. 8, 9.

2　　　　　　　　　　　　　A Mag-

A Magdalen, in tears, found grace,
    Yea a Manaſſeh's ſigh.
From Peter did he turn his face?
    O clemency, ſo high!

[b] Did he not yield his deareſt child,
    For rebel men, to die?
Will he not now be reconcil'd?
    O clemency, ſo high!

[i] Or fails the value of that blood
    For mercy ſtill to cry?
Has he forgotten to be good?
    O clemency, ſo high!

Ah! if he will my much forgive [k],
    Whoſe love ſhall mine outvie?
Him I will ſing, to him will live.
    O clemency, ſo high!

Riſe, riſe my ſoul, his goodneſs praiſe,
    And on his truth rely:
Jeſus th' eternal bond [l] diſplays.
    O clemency, ſo high!

---

[b] Rom. v. 6—10.   [i] Heb. xii. 24. ix. 14.
[k] Luke vii. 47.   [l] Heb. xiii. 20.

LII.

TRUST IN THE PROMISE OF DIVINE ASSISTANCE.

O Folly, chief in folly's ſhame!
  O baſeneſs, of the baſeſt name!
Him to reſiſt, reſiſting grieve [m],
Who ſought thy miſery to relieve;

Show'd thee thy ſins [n], thy danger ſhow'd,
Warn'd to eſcape, diſplay'd the road;
And, with his gentle touches, ſtrove
To win poſſeſſion of thy love.

Illuminating Spirit, ſhine
Once more; and make my ſoul thy ſhrine [o]:
Thy work of ſanctity revive [p],
Once more with me unworthy ſtrive [q].

---

[m] Acts vii. 51. Epheſ. iv. 30.   [n] John xvi. 8.
[o] Rom. viii. 9.   [p] 2 Theſſ. ii. 13.   1 Pet. i, 2.
[q] Gen. vi. 3.

I fear

I fear he will not : dark, forlorn,
With tears I've woo'd him to return :
He ſtands aloof ; though ſtill I pray.
O inſupportable delay !

Ah ! how ſhall I, thus left alone,
O'ercome my ſins now ſtronger grown?
How gain that faith ᶦ, whoſe ſtrength ſubdues
The world with all its tempting views ᵖ ?

How, ever, ſhall my ſoul poſſeſs
The placid joys of righteouſneſs ;
The cheering hopes, the pure deſires,
And all which love to God inſpires ?

I hear, I hear a gentle voice ;
" Rejoice, dejected ſoul, rejoice.
" 'Tis mine the ſpirit to beſtow ᶦ,
" The glorious purchaſe of my woe.

––––––––––––––––––

ᶦ Epheſ. ii. 8.   ᵖ 1 John v. 4.
ᶦ John xiv. 26, xv. 26. xvi. 7.   Rom. viii. 9.

" My

" My Father glorifies my name,
" From him this high donation came ".
" Aſk, ſeek, purſue ; the noble boon
" Shall crown thy ardent wiſhes ſoon ᵂ."

My ſoul, thy drooping courage raiſe,
Prepare, prepare the ſong of praiſe;
And, ſhaking off the mourner's duſt,
Fulfillment of the promiſe truſt.

LIII.

FEAR OF GOD.

TREMENDOUS Author of our frame,
    Holy and rev'rend is thy name ˣ.
Where in the ranks of Being round
Can, mighty God, thy peer be found ʸ?

ᵃ John xvi. 14.   Acts ii. 33. iii. 13.
ᵂ Matt. vii. 7, 8, 11. Luke xi. 13.   -   ˣ Pſalm
cxi. 9.   ʸ Iſaiah xl. 25.

High

High Lord of life and King of death,
Worlds rife and vanifh at thy breath [z].
Thou humbleft thy majeftic fight,
To view a Seraph and a mite [a].

The nations, in thy lofty eye,
Are nothing, lefs than vanity [b].
Who againft thee fhall lift his hand ?
Againft thy terrors who can ftand [c] ?

But, O how bleft, moft gracious Lord,
The fouls that tremble at thy word;
Thy anger to inflame afraid,
In noon-day beam and midnight fhade;

The fouls, whom rev'rence of thy will
Keeps from the bounding line of ill.
With fuch thy dwelling [d] is; on thofe
Thy peace its filling joys beftows.

----

[z] Pfalm LXVIII. 20.
[b] Ifaiah XL. 17.
[d] Ifaiah LVII. 15.

[a] Pfalm CXIII. 6.
[c] Job XLI. 10.

Thy

Thy wifdom guides [e], thy pow'r defends
Their life, till life its journey ends [f]:
Death fhall convey them to the land
Where all thy faints before thee ftand [g],

O that my foul with awful fenfe
Of thy tranfcendent excellence,
May clofe the day, the day begin ;
Jealous of every budding fin [h].

Never, O never, from my heart
May this great principle depart:
But act with unrelaxing pow'r
Within me, to my mortal hour.

———————————

[e] Pfalm xxv. 12, 14.   [f] Pfalm xxxi. 19, 20.
Heb xiii. 5.   [g] Ifaiah lvii. 1, 2. Pfalm i. 5.
    [h] Prov. xxiii. 17.

LIV.

TRUST IN DIVINE PROVIDENCE.

ANXIOUS cares and boding fears,
   Vexers of my foul, away.
'Tis not chance that rolls the fpheres,
   'Tis not chance that rules the day.

Who to man his lot decides ?
   He that man and all things made.
Who the good and ill divides ?
   He that form'd the light and fhade [i].

Can thy painful thought increafe
   In thy height a fingle fpan [k] ?
Yet thy life uphold in peace?
   Is all that the work of man ?

Foolifh mortals, bend your toil
   Heav'nly treafure to fecure:
Then, upon this earthly foil,
   Of all needful things be fure [l].

---

[i] Ifaiah XLV. 7.   [k] Matt. VI. 27.   Luke XII.
25, 26.   [l] Matt. VI. 33.

Well

Well, your heav'nly Father knows
   For your wants the fit supply [m]:
He on you his heav'n bestows [n] :
   Will he meat on earth deny ?

Dread not slander, nor disease [o],
   Safe beneath almighty shade :
If your proving he decrees,
   Trust in his supporting aid.

Not a sparrow falls to earth [p],
   Without God's permissive will :
Far exceeding is your worth,
   Who his holy laws fulfill.

Child of God, in death's dark vale [q]
   On thy father's goodness lean :
He will ne'er his children leave,
   In their last and trying scene.

---

[m] Matt. vi. 32.   [n] Luke xii. 32.
[o] Job v. 21.   Psalm xci. 3—7.
[p] Luke xii. 7.   [q] Psalm xxiii. 4. Heb. xiii. 5.

LV.

SELF-DEPENDENCE.

GOD reigns: Events in order flow,
　　Man's induſtry to guide [r];
But in a diff'rent channel go,
　　To humble human pride.

The ſwift not always, in the race,
　　Shall ſeize the crowning prize:
Not always wealth and honour grace
　　The labour of the wife [s].

Fond mortals but themſelves beguile,
　　While on themſelves they reſt.
Blind is their wiſdom, weak their toil,
　　By thee, O Lord, unbleſt [t].

----

[r] Prov. x. 4.　　　[s] Ecclef. IX. 11.
[t] Pſalm cxxvii. 1.

Go,

Go, hufbandman, the foil prepare,
　　Caft in the precious grain.
To thee belongs the fun, and air ?
　　Doft thou command the rain ?

Ye crafty, fcheme your winding way,
　　God fhall confound your fkill [u] :
Know, time and accident obey
　　His all-directing will.

Evil and good before him ftand,
　　His miffion to perform :　　　•
The bleffing comes at his command,
　　At his command the ftorm.

O Lord, in all our ways we'll own
　　Thy providential pow'r [x];
Intrufting to thy care alone
　　The lot of every hour.

----

[u] Job. v. 12.　　　[x] Prov. iii. 5, 6.

LVI.

PROSPERITY.

RICHES, in copious ſtreams,
   From every quarter flow :
Not one of all my fertile ſchemes
   Feels an abortive throe.

  My freighted veſſels ſail
   A length of ocean o'er ; ·
And bring me, with a ſpeeding gale,
   New wealth from every ſhore.

  My ſoul, thy warm deſires
   Indulge in all delight ᵞ.
Seize whatſoe'er thy fancy fires,
   Or raviſhes thy ſight.

  Roll in the gilded car,
   The rural palace rear :
There every gate, and opening, bar
   To charity and fear.

ᵞ Luke xii. 19.

Bid

Bid Luxury employ
Her ſkill, thy taſte to pleaſe.
Call thy rich friends to ſhare the joy [z],
And ſwim in mirth and eaſe.

To-day, in jocund bowls
Drown, drown forecaſting thought:
The morrow leave to gloomy ſouls,]
Who dread they know not what.

Thou fool, thy ſoul this eve [a]
Stern ſummons ſhall demand.
Whoſe name ſhall then thy houſe receive?
For whom thy coffers ſtand ?

------

[z] Luke xiv. 12.   [a] Luke xii. 20.

LVII.

WORLDLY-MINDEDNESS.

YE flefhly lufts, ye greedy cares
    For this frail mafs of clay;
For life which every pulfe impairs,
    For joys which pafs away;

No more my fimple heart inflave,
    No more my time confume.
Your works are finifh'd in the grave,
    Your pleafures in the tomb.

But Oh! beyond the tomb there lies
    The dungeon of defpair:
Thither the flefhly fpirit flies,
    To dwell in darknefs there.

The guilty fpirit there fhall quake,
    With fouls of kindred fin:
Till wrath's loud voice their duft awake,
    New fuff'rings to begin.

Then

Then fhall the lake of fulphur blaze,
    Fir'd by avenging breath ;
On them its quenchlefs fury preys—.
    Behold the *fecond death* [b] *!*

Awful feverity ! O fear,
    Worldlings, your Maker's hate [c].
His mercy's timely warnings hear,
    Left weeping come too late.

LVIII.

THE RICH EPICURE [d].

IS this the man, on earth fo gay ?
    In fplendor, there, and rich array,
With daily feaft and pamper'd eafe,
He ftudy'd every fenfe to pleafe.

---

[b] Rom. viii. 6. Revel. xxi. 8.
[c] Pfalm v. 5. Ifaiah xxvii. 11.
[d] Luke xvi. 19, &c.

Alas,

Alas, how chang'd! now doom'd to dwell
In the devouring flames of hell.
All wild with pain, he lifts his eyes
Up to the hills of paradife.

There he beholds at Abraham's fide
The lazar, who of hunger dy'd;
Whofe fruitlefs cries had oft implor'd
The offals of his wafteful board.

O Father Abraham, he faid;
" Send, fend, in mercy, to my aid
" Good Lazarus, to cool my tongue;
" With flame and raging thirft I'm ftung."

The patriarch fpoke: Thy good, my fon,
Is paft; on earth its courfe was run.
Paft are the ills, which Laz'rus bore;
The beggar Laz'rus weeps no more.

By equal retribution, know,
His lot is joy, but thine is woe.
Unpaffable, by fix'd decree,
Is the deep gulf 'tween us and thee.

I

LIX.

ADVERSITY.

HOW high our fanguine hopes we raife!
   How hotly our defires purfue
What fancy's magic glafs difplays
   Enlarg'd, and tempting to the view!

Thefe mortal objects of our love
   Too clofely twine about our heart,
Seduce our fouls from things above,
   And hardly leave to God a part.

O bitter change! when Heav'n's kind hand
   Snatches the fatal joy away,
Our feeble reafon fcarce can ftand
   Firm, in affliction's ftormy day.

We weep, we laugh, in mad extreme;
   Here, all delight; all fadnefs, there:
Now on the mount of blifs we feem,
   Now in the quagmire of defpair.

Stoics,

Stoics, who on your ftrength prefume,
 Could all your toiling wifdom find
A light to cheer affliction's gloom,
 A balfam for the wounded mind?

In vain you hail him good and great,
 Whofe ftedfaft foul no ills can move;
Boaft him impregnable to fate,
 And equal to your mighty Jove.

Jefus, our aking hearts we bring
 To learn philofophy from thee.
Thy words can make the mourner fing,
 And grief become a jubilee ᵉ.

Vain world, whofe fcenes of blifs and woe
 Are fhifting every fleeting hour ;
No longer fhall our fpirits owe
 Their peace, or trouble, to thy pow'r.

Teach us, thou Comforter divine,
 Contentment ; fhould our all be gone :
Teach us fubmiffion meek as thine,
 “ Father thy will, not mine, be done.”

ᵉ Matt. xi. 28—30. John xiv. 27.

I 2

LX.

RESIGNATION.

NEW to the fea of life, with eafy fail
　　(Smooth was the wave and bright the day)
My gilded bark before the fav'ring gale,
　　Freighted with pleafure, fkimm'd its way.

Fallacious fcene! in fulnefs of delight
ı　The heav'ns with fudden darknefs frown'd :
The ftorm came thundering down, in one black
　　　night
　　All, all my flatt'ring hopes were drown'd.

O why fo fwift the ftroke, and fo fevere ?
　　Whofe forrow can compare with mine?
Unwarn'd, undifciplin'd to changes here,
　　Muft I at once my all refign ?

Why

Why not refign ? the blefling was but lent,
   Its ufe but for a feafon giv'n ;
His the fole title who the blefling fent,
   Now only render'd back to Heav'n f.

Too rich a treafure to be long poflefs'd !
   'Twas happinefs, alas too great !
Enjoyment high, with fond embrace carefs'd
   Too ardent for a mortal ftate.

O how this faithlefs world has' chang'd its face !
   How poor appears the blifs of kings !
O worft of lunacy, for fouls to place
   Their all in perifhable things !

Short is the time, ere time fhall be no more ;
   And earth and all its works fhall die :
Far fhorter, ere to me this fcene be o'er ;
   Shifted to vaft eternity g.

---

f Job i. 21.   g i Cor. vii. 31.

I 3   Why

Why then thefe fruitlefs tears, and wafting fighs?
 Come, faith, and mount me on thy wing:
Bear me, O bear me, far beyond the fkies,
 To worlds where joys immortal fpring [h].

❀❀❀❀❀❀❀❀❀❀❀❀❀❀❀❀❀❀❀

LXI.

VICISSITUDE; OR,
JOY AFTER SORROW.

NOT always will the fky pour down,
 From fullen clouds, thefe fluicy rains;
Which every pleafing landfkip drown,
 And fadden and deform the plains.

Not always fhall the foreft groan
 With fhatt'ring winds; the mourning trees
Ever their leaflefs arms bemoan:
 Nor ftorm perpetual vex the feas.

---

[h] 2 Corinth. iv. 17, 18.

O

On rugged winter treads the fpring,
   That gentle feafon of delight:
And darknefs flees before the wing
   Of morn, infus'd in golden light.

Thus in the varying times of man,
   Which God's eternal counfel guides;
Smiles follow weeping, in the plan [i],
   By law unerring as the tides.

Should now the Heav'n-directed wheel
   Aloft our adverfe moments raife;
Onward, behind, the profp'ring fteal,
   Promife of joy-revolving days.

Mortal, adapt thy pliant mind [k]
   To all the changes that are giv'n;
Wifely rejoicing, or refign'd,
   Ne'er ftrive againft the fchemes of Heav'n.

---

[i] Ecclefiaftes III. 4.   [k] Ecclefiaftes VII. 14.

LXII.

FAITH IN GOD

WHY does my coward heart
  Yield up itſelf to *fear?*
Why thus at diſtant danger ſtart,
  And die when danger's near ?

Shall faith let go her hold?
Faith makes the tim'rous brave [l].
Is the Almighty arm grown old,
  And impotent to ſave [m] ?

---

[l] Heb. xi. 34.   [m] Iſaiah l. 2.

Why

Why thus difquieted, my foul [n],
   By hopelefs *grief* devour'd ;
When waves on waves of trouble roll,
   In ftorms around thee pour'd?

Hope thou in God ; He'll not difdain
   His children in diftrefs :
His hand their burden will fuftain,
   His grace their forrows blefs.

Ah ! could I hope, that He
   My foul has reconcil'd [o] ;
Courage would fpring and joy, in me
   His much-offending child.

His powerful love, I know,
   Is watchful o'er the juft.
Virtue is all he loves below [p],
   The reft is drofs and duft.

------

[n] Pfalm XLII. 5, 11.   [o] 2 Corinth. v. 19.
Rom. v. 10.   [p] Pfalm XXXIII. 13—18. Pfalm
XXXIV. 15, 16. Pfal. CXIX. 119.

4. O

O Thou, whoſe glory is to break
  Sin's miſerable chain [q],
Jeſus, my reſcue undertake,
  Me, me to virtue gain.

This deſert, then, I'll travel through
  Chearful, without diſmay;
Beholding, with the righteous few,
  The leader of our way [r].

---

[q] Luke IV. 18, 21. John VIII. 36.
[r] Heb. XII. 2.

LXIII.

CARE OF THE SOUL.

WHY came I here? What have I done,
  Since life began its race to run?
Have I been thoughtlefs of the goal,   ,
Following the inconfiderate fhoal,
     And ruining my foul?

Why thus for trifles will I ftrive?
Is it for trifles that I live?
Trifles my weak affections ftole.
Thefe trifles fhall I make my whole?
     For thefe exchange my foul?

In pleafure will I melt my days?
Hate ferious thought and ferious ways?
In mirth's perpetual circle roll,
Cards, fhows, and dances, and the bowl;
     Till I have loft my foul?

        I'll

I'll fwell my bags with golden ftore :
I'll count my fpreading acres o'er.
What though they fpread from pole to pole,
Where is the lucre of the whole,

     If purchas'd with my foul [s] *?*

Spring up, and foar, with vigorous wings,
Above thefe fublunary things :
To fenfual worldlings leave the whole,
To fools fhort-fighted as the mole.

     Be mindful of thy foul.

. Be ferious ere it is too late,
 Redeem for heav'n probation's ftate,
 Let God's commands thy life control,
 Then nothing fear beyond the goal.

    [t] *Save thy immortal foul.*

------

[s] Mark viii. 36. [t] Ezek. xviii. 27.

LXIV.

THE IMPORTANCE OF TIME.

TIME, Time, how few thy value weigh!
　How few will eftimate a day[a]!
Days, months and years keep rolling on,
The foul neglected and undone.

In painful cares, or empty joys,
Our life its precious hours deftroys :
While death ftands watching at our fide,
Eager to ftop the living tide.

Was it for this, ye mortal race,
The Maker gave you here a place?
Was it for this, his thought defign'd
The frame of your immortal mind?

---

[a] Ephef. v. 16, 17.　Ecclef. ix. 10.

For

For lofty cares, for joys fublime,
He fashion'd you the fons of time;
Pilgrims of time, ere long to be
The dwellers in eternity.

This feafon of your being, know,
Is portion'd you your deeds to fow.
Wifdom's and folly's differing grain
In future worlds is blifs and pain ^w.

Be warn'd.   Each night the day review,
Idle, or bufy ; fearch it through :
And while probation's minutes laft,
Let every day amend the paft.

————————————————

^w Gal. vi. 7, 8.

LXV.

THE TIME OF PROBATION.

" **B**Y my own endlefs life I fwear ˣ "
    (Strange language of almighty breath!)
" My bowels of compaffion fhare
   " No pleafure in a finner's death.

" O that the wicked would forfake
   " The guilty tenor of his ways!
" Turn, turn ye, of my grace partake;
   " Salvation ftill it's joys difplays."

Mercy, the time appointed, waits ʳ
   The time of trial meet for all :
And heav'n, unfolding wide her gates,
   Rejoices in the gracious call.

ˣ Fzek. xxxiii. 11.
ʳ Ifaiah xxx. 18. 2 Pet. iii. 9.

Warnings

Warnings divine forbid delay,
   And confcience cries aloud ; return,
While life's warm current works its way,
   Still gufhing from its tender urn,

Momentous feafon ! fhort, or long,
   As God's impartial will decides ;
Who, clear of cruelty and wrong,
   To every man its bound divides.

Sinner, *thy* feafon is unknown
   To thee, no fubject of thy pow'r.
Rafh finner, wilt thou dare poftpone
   Repentance to fome diftant hour ?

Should e'er that diftant hour arrive,
   More yielding will thy paffions grow [z] ?
And weaker thou, victorious ftrive
   Againft thy ftrong augmented foe ?

Ingrate ! will thus thy ftubborn heart
   Long-fuffering lenity withftand ?
Thus God's benignant counfels thwart ?
   Thus force down his deftroying hand ?

---

[z] Heb. III. 13. IV. 7.

His

His goodnefs if thou wilt defpife,

   His aggravated vengeance dread ;

When he in boundlefs wrath will rife,

   And pour his terrors on thy head [a].

LXVI.

TEMPTATION BY THE DEVIL.

IS he, alas ! allow'd

   To range this earth at will ;

The prince of darknefs, with his crowd

   Of demons bent on ill?

   Is he, whofe envious guile

   Seduc'd incautious Eve [b],

Suffer'd to practice every wile

   Her offspring to deceive ?

---

[a] Rom. ii. 4, 5.   [b] 2 Corinth. xi. 3.
1 Corinth. vii. 5. Eph. vi. 11. Rev. xx. 3, 7, 8.

K

As

As the fierce lion prowls
For rapine, through the wood;
Does this fierce fpirit hunt our fouls [c],
Athirft for human blood [d]?

Can he prefent the charm
That will our paffions fire [e]?
Our bofoms can his fury ftorm
With criminal defire?

Myfterious, mournful ftate
Of man beneath the fun!
But who a claim will arrogate,
To blame what God has done?

Children, your Father's name
In thankful fong refound.
The great Redeemer fing, who came
Your enemy to confound [f].

---

[c] 1 Pet. v. 8.   [d] John VIII. 44.
[e] Luke XXII. 3, 31.
[f] 1 John III. 8.

Truft

Truſt in his pow'r, confide
In his benevolent heart.
By the bold tempter he was try'd,
He baffled all his art ᵍ.

Truſt in his promiſe; ſtand,
Reſolv'd, againſt the foe:
The coward, at his dread command,
Shall flee to hell below ʰ.

LXVII.

INTEGRITY TOWARDS GOD.

AH! what avail's confeſſion's tongue,
    Without compunction's ſmart?
What value in thankſgiving ſong,
    Without a thankful heart?

ᵍ Matt. iv. 1, &c.   Heb. ii. 18.
ʰ 1 Pet. v. 9.   James iv. 7.

What

What is the virtue, which untry'd
    From vicious taint is pure ?
Gold will the fiery proof abide,
    And truth the teft endure.

Glorious Integrity ! which loves
    Thee, Lord, alone to pleafe [i]:
Which its unfeign'd devotion proves,
    In trouble and in eafe:

Which, when temptations fwarm around,
    Refifts ; and looks to thee :
And, nobly firm, maintains its ground.
    Glorious Integrity !

Which nourifhes no favourite fin [k],
    To all obedience free [l];
Zealous of fanctity within.
    Glorious Integrity !

---

[i] John xii. 43.   Gal. i. 10.   1 Theff. ii. 4.
[k] Pfalm xix. 12.
[l] Pfalm cxix. 6. cxxxix. 23, 24.

O happy

O happy they! whose conscience clear
   To thy atteft can flee [m],
In every strait and every fear.
   Glorious Integrity!

To these, thy condescending throne
   Allows their humble plea [n]:
These, as thy treasure thou wilt own [o].
   Glorious Integrity!

✿✿✿✿✿✿✿✿✿✿✿✿✿✿✿✿✿✿✿✿✿✿

LXVIII.

INTEGRITY's APPEAL TO JESUS CHRIST.

JESUS, to whose all-seeing eye
   My foes, my fears, my wants, are known;
In wants, in fears, from foes I fly,
For refuge, to thy pow'rful throne.

---

[m] Job xvi. 19. 2 Corinth. i. 8, 12.
[n] Pfalm xxxiv. 15. Prov. xv. 8.
[o] Malach. iii. 17.

K 3

Thy

Thy face, whofe beams like lightning dart
  On open guilt and cover'd guile;
Cheers with foft rays the upright heart,
  And fheds a heav'n in every fmile.

To thee, O Lord, my humble breaft
  Appeals for its integrity[p].
All guile, all evil I deteft,
  Glowing with grateful love to thee.

Thy anger worfe than death I fear,
  Thy favour more than life I prize.
O let my right in thee be clear,
  I'll fpurn at all beneath the fkies.

---

[p] John 11. 25. XXI. 15. Rev. 11. 23.

LXIX.

INTEGRITY

IN SEARCHING FOR DIVINE TRUTH.

MASTER divine, with docile hearts we bring
    Our reafon to receive thy light[q].
Bright as unclouded morn thy words fhall fpring,
    And fweetly chafe away our night.

Pure from its holy well, our fouls will draw
    Salvation's everlafting ftream.
No mortal names our heav'nly faith fhall awe[r],
    Vain their difpleafure and efteem.

But O how childhood's wrongly-tutor'd age
    Chains for the future man prepares[s]!
Our manhood from thofe fetters difengage,
    And free from fuperftition's fears.

---

[q] Luke xii. 56, 57. Acts xvii. 11.
[r] Matt. xxiii. 10. John vii. 48. 2 Corinth.
i. 24. 1 Pet. v. 3.   [s] John i. 46. vii. 27.

        When

When human pride thy humbling truths arraigns,
   May we to clear conviction bow :
Our flefhly lufts whene'er thy page reftrains [t],
   May we unfeign'd fubmiffion vow.

Come friendly Spirit, lead our fearching thought [u];
   All neceffary truth reveal :
And every truth, deep in our bofoms wrought,
   Stamp with thy fanctifying feal.

LXX.

INTEGRITY's IMPROVEMENT OF THE MEANS OF DIVINE KNOWLEGE.

THE more thy gofpel is furvey'd,
   Bleft Jefus, I the more approve.
Thy truths, thy law, thy promife weigh'd [w],
   I fix my faith, my hope, my love.

[t] John III. 19—21.   1 Corinth. II. 14.
[u] John VII. 17. XVII. 17.   Ephef. I. 17, &c.
[w] Luke XIV. 28—32.

                            Thus

Thus fix'd, unſhaken they remain;
   Cheriſh'd with thy nutritious care:
And fruit, from an immortal grain,
   Grateful to thee, O Father, bear [x].

Whether to thy creating will
   Nobler or meaner gifts I owe ;
May I my ſtewardſhip fulfil,
   May I in faith and goodneſs grow.

Water'd by nature's richeſt ſtreams,
   And by ſalvation's fountain fed ;
On vigorous root, beneath thy beams,
   Integrity exalts its head [y].

But though the toils of life opprcſs
   My days, and few thy gifts to me;
My humble rank of virtue bleſs :
   Thy love will bleſs integrity [z].

---

[x] Mark iv. 20. John xv. 1—5.
[y] Pſalm i. 3.
[z] Pſalm cxl. 13. Prov. xi. 20.

LXXI.

EQUITY OF THE DIVINE DISPENSATIONS.

WHO, gracious Father, ſhall complain
    Under thy mild and equal reign [a] ?
Who does a weight of duty ſhare,
More than his powers and aids can bear ?

With differing climes, and differing lands,
With fertile plains, and barren ſands,
Thy wiſdom form'd this earthy round,
And ſet the nations in their bound [b].

Varied alike, thy moral ray
Here ſheds a full, there fainter day [c].
The God of all, unkind to none,
To all the path of life has ſhown [d].

---

[a] Jer. ix. 24. Pſalm xxxiii. 5.   [b] Acts xvii. 26.
[c] Pſalm xxxiii. 12. cxlvii. 19, 20. Rom. i. 20. ii. 14.
[d] Pſalm cxlv. 9. Acts xvii. 27. xiv. 17.

A   What

What if a people for his praife [e]
He form, and high in virtue raife
For high reward ? Selected race,
Rejoice in this diftinguifh'd grace.

Rejoice ; but O with holy fear,
With toil unwearied and fevere,
Salvation's arduous work purfue [f],
And keep th' immortal crown in view.

Large is the bounty of his hand,
He will a large return demand [g].
Numbers will *wifh* to enter in,
But few the gate of heaven will *win* [h].

---

[e] Matt. v. 3—11, 14—16, 44—48. Eph. 1. 4—6.
1 Pet. 11. 9.   [f] Philip. 11. 12.
  [g] Luke xii. 48.   [h] Luke xiii. 24. Matt.
xi. 12. Luke xvi. 16.

LXXII.

GOVERNMENT OF THE BODY.

M Y body's curious frame,
    Full of wonders in each part,
O Lord, extols thy name;
Texture of thy fovereign art[i].

Shall I, alas! abufe
Organs of fuch noble worth?
    Service to thee refufe
Slave to appetites of earth[k]?

Did not the Son of God
Dignify this work of clay?
    Our mortal ground he trod,
Mortality his array.

---

[i] Pfalm cxxxix. 15—16.
[k] Rom. vi. 12,13.

That

That which he rais'd fo high,
I never more will difgrace:
    Never to fin's employ
Thefe honour'd members debafe.

    The bodies of the juft
For fhrines of glory defign'd,
    Shall awake from the duft,
Like their glorious Lord's refin'd [l].

    O let my foul afpire
A blifs fo great to fecure:
    It will my ardour fire
To keep my body all pure [m].

---

[l] Philip. III. 21.   [m] Coloff. III. 4, 5:

LXXIII.

CHASTITY.

IMPURE defires, flee far away[n];
   You that deflower the mind,
Ye fordid pleafures of a day
   With lafting pain behind;

Ye fogs, which from corruption rife,
   Eclipfing reafon's light:
Which good and evil, truth and lies,
   Confound in hellifh night[o].

O alien from all good, from God
   Wide wand'ring and eftrang'd!
In veftal fouls He makes abode,
   With energy unchang'd.

---

[n] 2 Corinth. vii. 1.   James i. 21.
[o] Rom. i. 26—28.

While

While o'er the facred page they bend,
　　Truth beams from every line:
And wonders, opening without end,
　　Tranfporting profpect! fhine.

Beneath the ftrong enliv'ning ray,
　　Immortal vigour grows.
Immortal hopes the growth repay,
　　And heav'nly fcenes difclofe.

Earth, at the voice which fhakes the fky,
　　Gives up her quick'ning mold:
The pure fhall then, with angel-eye,
　　The face of God behold P.

──────────

ᴾ Matt. v. 8.

LXXIV.

SPIRITUAL APPETITES AND GRATIFICATIONS.

POOR were the pleasures of the feast
   Perfia's high monarch held;
Though all the luxury of the east
   The fumptuous banquet fwell'd ^q.

The lufcious difh and flavorous bowl
   A flafh of rapture give:
But ftarving, dying, is the foul;
   Only the fenfes live.

Raife nobler appetites in me,
   My God, exalt my tafte;
Thy will my meal, and hope in thee
   My feftival repaft ^r.

----

q Efther I. 3, &c.
r Job xxiii. 12. John iv. 32, 34.

There

There vaſt unlimited deſires
    Untir'd fruition find.
Fruition ſtill new thirſt inſpires,
    For new delights deſign'd [s].

There lively and heart-ſtrength'ning joys
    From ſelf-inſpection flow [t];
While life divine each hour employs;
    A paradiſe below!

With meditation's wing the ſoul
    Springs, up th' eternal hills:
At length, the ſtars beneath her roll,
    And heav'n her bliſs fulfills.

---

[s] Pſalm xxxvi. 8, 9. xxxvii. 4.   Matt. v. 6.
[t] Prov. xiv. 14. xv. 15.

L

LXXV.

GOVERNMENT OF THE MIND.

IMPERIAL reafon, hold thy throne.
   Confcience, to cenfure and approve
To thee belongs. Ye paffions, own
   Subjection, and in order move.

Inchanting order! peace how fweet!
   Delicious harmony within!
Bleft felf-command, thy pow'r I greet.
   Ah! when fhall I fuch empire win?

The hero's laurel fades, the fame
   For boundlefs fcience is but wind,
And Sampfon's ftrength a brutal name,
   Without dominion of the mind.

Sampfon

Sampſon behold, a harlot's ſlave!
   The warlike David fell by love.
Vaſt knowledge fail'd his ſon to ſave [u]
   From bowing [w] in Aſtarte's [x] grove.

The beauty and the pow'rful arms
   Of ſelf-command, in juvenile fire,
See; when the miſtreſs ſpreads her charms
   And tempts in vain her ſlave's deſire [y].

But, of all patterns moſt ſublime,
   Jeſus, on thee I love to gaze.
O ſelf-command, to wond'ring time
   Unknown in old and modern days!

Thy holy mind in reaſon ſtrong,
   With paſſions regular and pure,
Pity'd the mighty and the throng,
   In native dignity ſecure.

---

[u] 1 Kings iv. 29—34.   [w] 2 Kings v. 18.
[x] Aſhtoreth (the moon) the Goddeſs of the Zidonians,
1 Kings xi. 2—8, 2 Kings xxiii. 13.
[y] Gen. xxxix. 7—12.

L 2   Not

Not offer of imperial pow'r [z],
 Nor flattery's praise [a], nor foul difgrace [b],
Nor cruel death's advancing hour [c],
 Alter'd one feature in thy face.

Serene as heav'n, thy ftedfaft zeal
 Duty with dazzling luftre crown'd :
Till thy great work, to teach and heal,
 Had meafur'd its appointed bound [d].

With trembling feet, at diftance I
 Thy glorious footfteps would purfue.
Grant, that in me the marking eye
 A fketch of felf-command may view.

---

[z] Matt. iv. 8, 9, 10. John vi. 15.
[a] Matt. xxii. 16. Luke ix. 43, 44.
[b] Matt. ix. 24. Luke xvi. 14. John viii. 48, 49.
[c] Mark x. 32—34. Luke ix. 51.
[d] Luke xiii. 32. John ix. 4.

LXXVI.

THE CONFLICT.

MY judgment, guided from above,
  Shows me the way of truth and reft;
Urges my ling'ring feet to move,
  And fmites reluctance in my breaft e.

Ah! wherefore do I not obey
  Thefe friendly warnings of my mind?
What drives my foolifh fteps aftray?
  Another foul perverfe and blind?

'Tis flefh, and lawlefs appetite;
  Thefe againft reafon's fway rebel:
Thefe to all ill my heart incite,
  Thefe the loud voice of confcience quell f.

---

e Rom. vii. 15, 16, 22.
f Rom. vii. 18. Gal. v, 17.

L 3   I ftruggle,

I ftruggle, but alas! in vain,
  Too oft in vain! with furious tide
My paffions rufhing down amain
  Too oft my beft refolves deride ᵍ.

Ah! wretched me! what pow'r fhall fave
  Me from the pow'r of fin and death?
Thou, thou alone, whofe mercy gave
  For captive ʰ men thy dying breath ⁱ.

Come, Jefus, with forgiving grace,
  Come, with thy fpirit and thy word;
My paft iniquities efface,
  And be my faviour and my Lord.

ᵍ Rom. VII. 19.   ʰ Rom. VII. 14, 23.
ⁱ Rom. VII. 24, 25. VIII. 1—3. Rom. v. 6, 8.

LXXVII.

KEEPING THE HEART.

SMILING pleaſures,
  Glitt'ring treaſures,
Spreading all their dangers round,
  Warn my ſteering,
  Always fearing,
As through life my courſe I found.

  Example alarms
  With vice's ſtrong arms ;
And faſhion's follies unite,
  To draw me away,
  From virtue's high way,
To ſin's illuſive delight.

  Senſe inviting,
  Paſſions fighting,
For indulgence of their joy ;
  Whither fleeing,
  Shall my Being,
Here, in ſafety time employ?

With

With diligent ward,
Each avenue guard
That opens accefs to the heart,
The fountain is there
Which, turbid or fair,
The ftreams to life will impart [k],

From defiring,
From admiring
Fruit unlawful, check thy thought.
Won by praifing,
And by gazing,
Eve to pluck the charm was brought [l],

Warm fancy withftand;
The work of her hand
To dafh, no minute delay.
Yea, ere fhe begin,
Her painting of fin,
Quick fnatch her pencil away.

---

[k] Prov. iv. 23,   [l] Gen. iii. 5, 6.

LXXVIII.

SELF-KNOWLEGE.

ALAS! too bufy to be wife,
  Or elfe in floth's amufements wand'ring;
We fcarce will ever turn our eyes
Upon ourfelves, with ferious pond'ring.

On ev'ry toy abroad we gaze,
Ourfelves we fhun, at home are ftrangers;
  And round and round in error's maze
We trifle on, eternal rangers.

If e'er, perchance, we look within,
Self-love, our fancy'd virtues pleading,
  Hoodwinks the judgment; lurking fin
And fwarming fpecks averfe from heeding.

Vain-glory hence, and fierce difdain
Of wife benevolent monition;
  Hence fury, when the Good arraign
Our envy, av'rice, or ambition [m].

---

[m] Prov. IX. 8. Matt. VII. 6.

Efta-

Eftablifh'd thus, ill habits grow
Too ftrong to yield to felf-correction;
   Too high for reafon (dreadful woe!)
To awe their frenzy to fubjection [a].

LXXIX.

THE SAME SUBJECT, IN A
DIFFERENT METRE.

YE fools, abroad you gáze round,
   But ftrángers ftill at hóme;
In váin amúfements wánd'ring,
   From tóy to tóy you roám.

Or fir'd with luft of lucre,
   In bufy fcenes you toil;
Devifing, and devifing,
   To dig the golden foil.

---

[a] Jer. XIII. 23.

Ah!

Ah! what kind vo'ce fhall win you,
　　Yourfelves, yourfelves, to know?
While thus you fhun your bofoms,
　　How faft your follies grow!

Of wife advice difdainful,
　　Too knowing to be taught;
You redden at the warning,
　　Which dares but hint a fault.

Self-love, alas, whenever
　　You glance upon your heart;
Connives at all your vices,
　　Or colours o'er with art.

Your pride is *confcious merit*;
　　- Ambition, *noble flame*;
And wrath, *quick fenfe of honour*;
　　And av'rice, *forefight*'s name.

Ill habits thus advancing,
　　Too high for reafon's rule,
Too ftrong for felf-correction,
　　Go live and die a fool.

LXXX.

DIVINE DISCIPLINE NECESSARY TO SELF-KNOWLEGE.

WHAT a perplexing wild
  Is ſelf-deluſion's art!
Who by himſelf is unbeguil'd?
  Who traces all his heart [o]?

To thee, O Lord, alone
  The myſt'ry lies reveal'd.
Our windings all to thee are known,
  And not a thought conceal'd [p].

With ſelf-applauſes vain,
  Few of our faults we ſee:
And for thoſe few we fondly feign
  Some ſelf-excuſing plea [q].

---

[o] Pſalm xix. 12. [p] Pſalm cxxxix. 2.
[q] Iſ. v. 20, 21. James i. 26.

Lord,

Lord, fearch me, prove me through:
By difcipline fevere :
And to myfelf my fpirit fhew,
From all difguifes clear.

If feeds of guilt and woe
Are cherifh'd in my breaft ;
Or if my feet unthinking go
In paths by thee unblefs'd ;

Expell the latent foes,
My quick return befriend '.
O lead me in the way which knows
No bitternefs nor end.

' Pfalm cxxxix. 23, 24.
' Pfalm cxix. 176.

LXXXI.

REPROOF.

TO felf-admiring folly burn
   The frankincenfe of lying praife ᵗ,
Let the proud fcorner's anger fpurn
   The friendly cenfor of his ways ᵘ.

Come parents, paftors, faithful friends;
   In merciful alliance join
To fmite me ʷ, when my *act* offends,
   Or when to evil I *incline.*

Your wounds are fanative; the fmart
   I welcome, 'tis a pleafing pain.
You lance the ulcer in my heart,
   Sweet health of mind by you I gain ˣ.

ᵗ Prov. xxvi. 28. xxix. 5.
ᵘ Prov. ix. 7, 8. xv. 12.
ʷ Pfalm cxli. 5.
ˣ Prov. vi. 23. xxvii. 5, 6.

Ye

Ye fools, why will your pride refuse
  The warning voice, the guiding hand?
Embrace rebuke, wife counfel chufe;
  Or perifh, with the froward Band ʳ.

✿✿✿✿✿✿✿✿✿✿✿✿✿✿✿✿✿✿✿✿✿✿✿

LXXXII.

-

P R I D E.

O Pride, thou dropfy of the mind,
  Of felf-delufion born;
Hateful to God ᶻ, by all mankind
  In others feen with fcorn.

Shall finning man, O Lord, prefume
  To glory in thy fight?
Himfelf on his own virtues plume ᵃ?
  And claim thy heav'n by right?

ʸ Prov. xv. 10, 32.
ᶻ Pfalm cxxxviii. 6. Ifaiah ii. 12.
ᵃ Luke xviii. 11, 12.

I boaft

I boaſt of none, in none I'll truſt,
    For mercy, Lord, I ſue [b].
Ah! were my judge ſeverely juſt,
    Perdition is my due [c].

Shall mortal man, ſo blind and weak,
    On his own pow'rs depend?
In thee I hope, thy bleſſing ſeek,
    O guide me and defend [d].

Shall man his brother man deſpiſe,
    Vain of excelling worth?
And view aſkance, with haughty eyes,
    His fellow worm of earth?

Who made my birth, or ſtation, high?
    Another's mean and low?
Who made that poor man's cup ſo dry,
    But mine to overflow [c]?

---

[b] Luke xviii. 13.   [c] Job ix. 2, 3. Pſalm cxxx,
3, 4. cxliii. 2.   [d] Prov. iii. 5, 6. Jer. ix. 23, 24,
[c] Prov. xxii. 2. Pſ. xxiii. 5.

My

My pride fhall nobler talents fwell ?
   Who made yon ideots fmall ?
Who gave me talents to excell ᶠ ?
   Who but the God of all ? .

O come, meek-ey'd Humility,
   Come, dwell within my breaft.
Thus, Jefus, I would learn of thee,
   And feel thy promis'd reft ᵍ.

✳✳✳✳✳✳✳✳✳✳✳✳✳✳✳✳✳✳✳✳✳✳✳✳✳✳✳✳✳

LXXXIII.

HUMILITY.

FIRST PART.

WAS pride, alas ! e'er made for man ʰ ?
   Blind, erring, guilty creature he,
His birth the duft, his life a fpan,
   His wifdom lefs than vanity.

ᶠ 1 Cor. iv. 6, 7.   ᵍ Matt. xi. 29.
ʰ Ecclefiafticus x. 18.

M

If wealth and pow'r with dazzling rays
   And pageant ſtate this nothing dreſs;
On the fair idol ſhall we gaze ?
   And envy *that* as happineſs ?

Jeſus, by thy inſtruction taught,
   Our fooliſh paſſions are repreſt :
We bluſh at our miſguided thought,
   And ſee and call the humble bleſt.

To know ourſelves, to learn of thee,
   And bend our necks beneath thy throne,
Thus dictates wiſe Humility,
   This makes the wealth of heav'n our own'.

₽ Matt. v. 3.

LXXXIV.

HUMILITY.

SECOND PART.

BLEST men, of lowly mind,
 In felf-opinion poor;
For you, what honour is defign'd!
 For you, what princely ftore ᵏ!

In time's fhort joys and fighs,
 Thankful, or meekly ftill;
Whate'er he gives you, or denies,
 You love your Father's will.

The high and holy One,
 Who all his works furveys,
Marks you, from his eternal throne,
 As temples to his praife ˡ.

ᵏ Matt. v. 3. Prov. xv. 25. xviii. 12. xxix. 23.
ˡ Ifaiah lvii. 15. 1 Cor. vi. 19. 2 Cor. vi. 16.
1 Pet. ii. 5.

To you, to you he bends
His condefcending ear [m] ;
To you his pow'rful arm extends,
In every want and fear.

From your mifgiving breaft
Sad diffidence remove.
Why, children, are your fouls depreft ?
Why doubt your Father's love ?

With mildnefs in his face,
Your weakneffes he views.
To humble worfhippers, his grace
He never will refufe [n].

From the proud pharifee
His countenance he turns:
But will not with difpleafure fee
A publican who mourns [o].

---

[m] Pfalm cii. 17. Prov. xv. 8.
[n] Pfalm cxxxviii. 6. Prov. iii. 34. 1 Pet. v. 5.
[o] Luke xviii. 9—14.

LXXXV.

MEEKNESS.

MEEKNESS, ally'd
　　To foft Humility,
The foot of Pride
Will never tread on thee.

　Patient of wrong,
To wrong canft thou incline?
　Gentlenefs of tongue,
And manners mild are thine.

　Iron is the breaft
Thy fweetnefs cannot charm;
　By fiends poffeft,
The man who works thy harm.

　Obdurate fteel
Is liquefy'd by flame:
　Malice will feel,
By thee, relenting fhame.

M 3

Envy

Envy will chain
Her fnakes; and fcandal's fpite,
  Blufhing, refrain
Thy harmlefs name to bite.

Cheerful thy days,
In fweet abode of peace;
  Crown'd with all praife,
Thy blifs fhall never ceafe [r].

LXXXVI.

ANGER AND MEEKNESS.

MARK, when tempeftuous winds arife,
    The wild confufion and uproar;
All ocean mixing with the fkies,
  And fhipwrecks dafh'd upon the fhore.

-----

[r] Matt. v. 5.

Not lefs confufion racks the mind,
   By its own fierce ideas toft ;
When reafon is to rage refign'd,
   And in the whirl of paffion loft.

O felf-tormenting child of Pride ^q,
   Anger, bred up in hate and ftrife ^r ;
Ten thoufand ills, by thee fupply'd,
   Mingle the cup of bitter life.

Happy the meek, whofe gentle breaft,
   Serene as fummer's evening ray,
Calm as the regions of the bleft,
   Enjoys on earth celeftial day.

No friendfhips broke ^s their bofoms fting,
   No jars their peaceful tents invade,
Safe underneath Almighty wing ^t,
   And, foes to none, of none afraid.

---

^q Prov. xxi. 24.   ^r Prov. xv. 18. xxviii. 25.
^s Prov. xxii. 24.
^t Pfalm lxxvi. 9. Ifaiah xi. 4.

Spirit of grace, all meek and mild,
   With thy whole felf our fouls poffefs :
Paffion and pride be hence exil'd,
   So fhall our frame thy own exprefs.

LXXXVII.

E N V Y.

MALIGNANT Envy, come not near,
   Some wretch of infamy torment.
Come not, to trouble my repofe,
   Thou fpawn of pride and difcontent.

Go, move the tempter to deftroy
   Some world of innocence again ᵘ.
Go, and another Abel find,
   To perifh by another Cain.

 ᵘ John vɪɪɪ. 44.   2 Corinth. xɪ. 3.   Wifd. ɪɪ. 24.

                            Or

Or fome hard-hearted brethren mould,
   A Jofeph's favourite life to fell [w].
Or fome delicious vineyard eye,
   And in a fecond Ahab dwell [x].

Yea, could the Son of God again
   Appear in fervile form below;
Inflame malevolence, once more
   To ftrike the crucifying blow [y].

Not blackeft night and brighteft noon
   Are with each other more at ftrife,
O Jefus, than the envious mind
   Is with thy Gofpel and thy life.

May I too humble be for pride,
   Too felf-contented to repine:
And too benevolent, to wifh
   My neighbour's bleffings lefs than mine.

---

[w] Gen. xxxvii. 11, 28,
[x] 1 Kings xxi. 1—16.
[y] Mark xv. 10.

'

LXXXVIII.

RELIGIOUS CONTENTMENT.

I Envy not the worldly Great,
  Their coftly viands and their pride of fhow,
Inchantment all; delufion's bait;
Fools rufh along, and plunge in death and woe.

Give me the peafant's clay-built cell,
On a coarfe pillow reft my weary head.
  If there with me my God will dwell,
With cheerful heart I'll blefs my homely bread [z],

The lofty majefty of God,
Who in eternity of Glory reigns,
  In vifits to a mean abode,
Defcends to commune with adoring fwains [a].

---

[z] Pfalm xxxvii. 16.   Prov. xv. 16. xvi. 8.
[a] Ifaiah lvii. 15.

5

O happy

O happy fouls, in humble feat [b]!
What tranfports from divine communion flow!
Angels will you as brethren greet,
And hail the type of their own heav'n below.

* *

LXXXIX.

MALEVOLENCE.

O Dreadful fcale of fin !
　　To wrath fee envy fwell ;
Fix'd wrath is hate, and all within
　　Malevolent as hell.

A fong inflam'd the Jealous Saul,
　　A Demon his dark foul poffefs'd :
The furious javelin pierc'd the wall,
　　But meant the envy'd David's breaft [c].

---

[b] 1 Tim. vi. 6.　　[c] 1 Sam. xviii. 6—11.

The

The victim he purfu'd
Mountains and deferts o'er;
Revenging charitable food,
With facerdotal gore [d].

Good heav'n! that e'er thy human race
Should thefe infernal paffions breed!
Deftroy thy image, and debafe
Their glory into Satan's feed [e]!

Ye friendly fouls, who burn
With love to human kind,
Whofe feelings, with abhorrence, turn
From the malignant mind;

The yoke of Jefus why decline?
Why caft his law of love away?
O come, nature's weak aid refign,
And bow beneath his gentle fway.

---

[d] 1 Sam. xxi. 1, 6. xxii. 9—19.
[e] John viii. 40, 44. 1 John iii. 8—12.

XC.

L O V E.

O God of love, thy glory
    Blazes in the gospel plan,
Abounding with the story
    Of thy flowing love to man.

High love, beyond conceiving,
    Gave thy sole-begotten son;
That the bliss of souls believing
    Should through endless ages run[f].

Warm with divinest feeling,
    Down the Filial Goodness came:
And, to mediate our healing,
    Bore a vile delinquent's shame[g].

---

[f] John iii. 16, 17. 1 John iv. 9, 10.
[g] John xv. 13. Gal. ii. 20. Ephes. iii. 17—19.
v. 25—27. Is. liii. 5, 12.

Who,

Who, Lord, thy name avowing
　Shall his glorious title prove?
Are not all of thy allowing
　Men of univerfal love [h].

Lo, my bofom is expanding
　To receive this heav'nly gueft;
All of human form demanding
　Friendly manfion in my breaft.

But where thy image beaming
　In my fellow man I fee;
My full affections ftreaming
　Pour their ftrongeft energy [i].

O Love, of all the Graces
　Faireft, thy fweet influence
Anger and pride effaces;
　Eafy to forgive offence.

---

[h] John xiii. 34, 35. Luke x. 27—37.
[i] Gal. vi. 10. 1 John iii. 16.

Well-

Well-spring of social blessings,
  Bearing, giving, soft and kind;
Sincere in thy caressings,
  Candid is thy gentle mind [k].

How charming is the union,
  By this noble virtue wrought!
How pleasant the communion,
  By this noble virtue taught!

This heightens ev'ry beauty
  In all other virtues found;
Endears each act of duty
  In the social circle's bound.

Hope ceases, by enjoyment;
  Faith shall fail, in vision's bliss;
Love endures; best employment
  In the world of happiness [l].

———————

[k] 1 Corinth. xiii. 4—7.
[l] 1 Corinth. xiii. 8, 13.

XCI.

UNCHARITABLE JUDGMENT.

ALL-KNOWING God, 'tis thine to know
    The fprings whence wrong opinions flow;
To judge, from principles within,
When frailty errs, and when we fin.

Who among men, high Lord of all,
Thy fervants to his bar may call?
Decide of herefy, and fhake
A brother o'er the flaming lake[m]?

Who with another's eye can read?
Or worfhip by another's creed?
Revering thy command alone,
We humbly feek and ufe our own[n].

---

[m] Rom. xiv. 4.   2 Corinth. i. 24.
[n] Matt. xxiii. 8—10.   John v. 39.   Acts xvii. 11.
1 Theff. v. 21.   1 John iv. 1.

If wrong, forgive; accept, if right;
While faithful we obey our light,
And, cens'ring none, are zealous ftill
To follow as to learn thy will°.

When fhall our happy eyes behold
Thy people fafhion'd in thy mold?
And charity our lineage prove
Deriv'd from thee, O God of love ᴾ?

❀❀❀❀❀❀❀❀❀❀❀❀❀❀❀❀❀❀❀❀❀❀❀

XCII.

PERSECUTION.

ABSURD and vain attempt! to bind
With iron chains the free-born mind;
To force conviction, and reclaim
The wand'ring by deftructive flame:

° John xiii. 17.   ᴾ ɪ John iv. 7.

N   Bold

Bold arrogance ! to snatch from Heav'n
Dominion not to mortals giv'n P ;
O'er conscience to usurp the throne,
Accountable to God alone.

Mad zeal ! that with hell-fury burns,
The rights of God and man o'erturns q :
Whose blind presumption sanctifies
Murders, rebellions, plots, and lies.

That fills the world with blood and woe,
That hurls down kingdoms at a blow,
That butchers souls, and peoples hell
With converts which its arms compell.

Thus Rome asserts her proud decrees,
Inforc'd by fierce anathemas ;
And wakens vengeance, to devour
The foes of Antichristian pow'r.

P 2 Theff. 11. 4.   1 Pet. v. 3.
q John xvi. 2.   Acts ix. 1. xxvi. 9—11.

Jesus,

Jefus, thy gentle law of love
Does no fuch cruelties approve ʳ.
Mild as thyfelf, thy doctrine wields
No arms but what perfwafion yields ˢ.

By proofs divine and reafon ftrong,
It draws the willing foul along;
And conquefts to thy church acquires,
By eloquence which heav'n infpires ᵗ.

O happy, who are thus compell'd
To the rich feaft by Jefus held ᵘ !
Britain, thy bleffings know; and prize
The light which liberty fupplies.

ʳ Luke ix. 54—56.
ˢ 2 Corinth. x. 3—5.
ᵗ 1 Corinth. ii. 4, 5, 13.
ᵘ Luke xiv. 23.

N 2

XCIII.

P R O B I T Y; or,
INTEGRITY TOWARDS MAN.

AS the limpid ſtream, which flows
  O'er a bed of golden ſand,
All its ſhining treaſure ſhows,
  Tempting the beholder's hand;

So the honeſt heart is ſeen,
  In the mild expanded eye,
In the open generous mien
  Of the man of probity.

In the honeſt heart abide,
  Truth with undeluding tongue ʷ,
Faith that never warps aſide,
  Thoughts which never mean a wrong.

ʷ Prov. XII. 17.

Who

Who, fuch treafure to poffefs,
    Feels not friendfhip's warm defire ?
Who the friendfhip will not blefs
    Glowing with fo pure a fire ?

In that ever trufty breaft,
    I with confidence repofe,
Secret as the houfe of reft,
    All my triumphs, all my woes.

But alas ! what happy clime
    Is for men of truth renown'd ?
Where, in all the walks of time,
    Was the precious bleffing found ?

Falfe and felfifh, ev'ry one
    Seeks his brother to deceive ˣ ;
Falfe the fmile, and falfe the groan ʸ,
    They are cheated who believe.

ˣ Pfalm v. 9. Ifaiah LIX. 13—15. Jer. VII. 28.
ʸ Pfalm XLI. 6. LV. 21.

God

God of truth, the lying phrafe,
　Of diffembling lips, to thee
Hateful is ; thou lov'ft the ways
　Of the man of probity [a].

XCIV.

HYPOCRISY TOWARDS MAN.

CONDITION hard of focial life,
　　When love and prudence are at ftrife!
While *that* the kindeft thoughts infpires [b],
This caution and diftruft requires.

Falfhood alas! too oft we meet,
And for a friend a Joab greet:
With fmiles and glozing fpeech careft
We feel the poniard in our breaft [c].

---

[z] Pfalm v. 6. LII. 2—5.　Prov. VI. 16, 17.
[a] Prov. XII. 22.　　　　[b] 1 Corinth. XIII. 4, 5.
[c] 2 Sam. III. 26, 27.

There are, who in my happy days
Will eat my bread and found my praife :
But when my feftal times are o'er,
Shun, as they would the plague, my door.

There is, whofe heart I fondly thought
In the fame mould with mine was wrought ;
To whom my fecret I unclos'd,
And my whole naked foul expos'd.

Ere long his falfhood he betray'd ;
He publifh'd counfels of the fhade
On the houfe-top : Yea join'd my foe,
And wove the plot to lay me low [d].

O for the pinions of a dove [e] !
Far from all traitors I'd remove :
And in fome lonely harmlefs wild,
Dwell there unknown and unbeguil'd.

O rather, Lord, thy fervant give
In love and wifdom here to live ;
Till thou indulge me a releafe
To thy own world of truth and peace.

---

[d] 2 Sam. xv. 31. Pfalm XLI. 9. LV. 12—14.
[e] Pfalm LV. 6.

N 4

XCV.

INOFFENSIVENESS.

WHILE in this world I dwell,
  The paths of fin I'll fear [f] :
And, pond'ring all my goings well,
  Walk inoffenfive here [g].

My ev'ry ftep I'll aim,
  As warn'd by wifdom's zeal [h] ;
Left e'er, O Lord, thy holy name
  By me a wound fhould feel [i].

To me let no man owe
  His hatred of thy ways.
From me let no man's forrow flow,
  The guilt of no man's days.

---

[f] Prov. xxviii. 14.   [g] Acts xxiv. 16,
1 Corinth. x. 32.   [h] Prov. xiv. 16. Eph. v. 15.
[i] 2 Sam. xii. 14.   1 Pet. iii. 16.

Nor

Nor will I rashly draw
Man's vengeance on my head,
By warmth untimely; when thy law
Under their feet they tread [k].

Thus blameless may I live [l],
Thus grace the faith I own [m];
Thus win ev'n infidels to give
Due honours to thy throne [n].

XCVI.

CHRISTIAN PRUDENCE AND FORTITUDE.

FATHER of lights [o], my footsteps guide
Along the dang'rous path I tread.
Ne'er suffer me to turn aside,
By error or by sin misled.

---

[k] Matt. vii. 6.   [l] Philipp. i. 10.
[m] Tit. ii. 10.   [n] Matt. v. 16.   1 Pet. iii. 16.
[o] James i. 17.

While

While the mad world around me spend,
    Their days in folly or in crime;
O that my feet may always tend,
    To wise redemption of my time ᴾ !

With truth illuminate my mind,
    Inspire with fortitude my heart:
Ne'er let me wander with the blind,
    Nor waver in the Christian's part.

Fashion and crowds conspire in vain,
    To shake the firmness of my soul ᑫ :
All your allurements I disdain,
    God only shall my choice control.

ᴾ Ephef. v. 15, 16.   ᑫ Exod. xxiii, 2.
Rcm. xii. 2. 1 John ii. 15, 16.

XCVII.

JUSTICE.

FORBID it, heav'n! that e'er I eat
    The bread of craftinefs and wrong [r],
A curfe would poifon all my meat,
    As fatal as the viper's tongue [s].

I ne'er will raife a poor man's figh,
    His hire fhall never fwell my ftore [t].
I dread the poor man's plaintive cry,
    I fear the father of the poor [u].

If I in darknefs (bafe mifdeed!)
    Affaffinate my neighbour's fame [w];
By me if innocency bleed,
    Cancel from earth my hated name [x].

---

[r] Prov. iv. 17.　　　[s] Job xx. 14—16.
[t] Prov. xxii. 16.　Mal. iii. 5.　James v. 4.
[u] Pfalm lxviii. 5.　Job xxxiv. 28.
[w] Pfalm l. 20. xi. 2.
[x] Pfalm lii. 2, 4, 5. ci. 5.

Ah!

Ah! no; let me with ſtrong delight
  To all the tax of duty pay;
Tender of every ſocial right,
  Revering thy all-righteous ſway.

Such virtue thou wilt ne'er forget,
  In worlds where every virtue ſhares
High recompence; though not of debt,
  But which thy bounteous grace prepares.

XCVIII.

MERCY.

BEHOLD a wretch in woe,
  A brother mortal mourns :
My eyes with tears, for tears, o'erflow,
My heart his ſighs returns [y].

---

[y] Rom. XII. 15.

I hear

I hear the thirfty cry,
The famifh'd beg for bread :
O let my fpring its ftream fupply,
My hand its bounty fhed [z].

Lo, the poor debtor fues,
Pale at the penal threat,
A ftarving family he fhews ;
I cancel all the debt [a].

And fhall not wrath relent,
Touch'd by that humble ftrain,
My brother crying, " I repent,
" Nor will offend again ?"

How elfe, on fprightly wing,
Can hope bear high my pray'r
Up to thy throne, my God, my king,
To plead for pardon there [b] ?

. [z] Job xxii. 7.   If. lviii. 7, 10.
  [a] Ezek. xviii. 7.   Matt. vi. 12.
  [b] Matt. vi. 14, 15. xviii. 23—35.

The

The pitiful and kind
Thy pity will repay.
With thee fhall the forgiving find
A fweet forgiving day [c].

But juftice lifts her fcale,
And fhakes her rod on high :
Nor pray'rs, nor fighs, nor tears avail
The fons of cruelty [d].

❁❁❁❁❁❁❁❁❁❁❁❁❁❁❁❁❁❁❁❁❁❁❁

XCIX.

SUMMARY OF CHRISTIAN VIRTUES, WITH THEIR BEATITUDES.

NOT all that pow'r affords,
Nor mirth that wine infpires,
Nor what fharp avarice hoards,
Or martial toil acquires ;
Not conquering arms,
Nor beauty's charms,
Can form the plan
Of blifs for man.

---

[c] 2 Sam. xxii. 26. Matt. v. 7.   [d] James ii. 13.

Happy

Happy *the humble minds* ᵉ,
In felf-opinion poor:
There faith a dwelling finds,
And brings her precious ftore.
 In heav'n enroll'd,
 A crown of gold
 Around their head
 Its blaze fhall fpread.

Happy, *who try'd in woes*
Welcome correction's pain;
Whofe tears *repentance* fows,
Rich feed ne'er fown in vain.
 A harveft fprings
 Of joyful things,
 Which God will keep
 For them to reap.

Happy *the meek*, whofe breaft
No angry paffion fhakes;
Of inward calm poffeft,
When tempeft round them breaks.

———————

ᵉ Matt. v. 3—12.

The

The wing of God,
O'er their abode,
Secure repofe
And peace beftows.

Happy the fouls renew'd,
Who *thirft* for wifdom's fpring,
And *hunger* for the food
Which virtue's banquets bring.
    They now fhall tafte
    The rich repaft;
    Then blifs intire
    Shall fill defire.

Happy the men whofe hearts
Relenting *mercy* fways:
Mercy which God imparts,
The merciful repays:
    He hears their cries,
    Their wants fupplies,
    Their pains relieves,
    Their fins forgives.

Happy

Happy the mind whofe eye
No clouds of *luſt* obfcure;
Whofe pow'rs can upward fly,
From vile affections *pure.*

 Thy ravifh'd fight,
 In worlds of light,
 On God fhall gaze,
 And drink his blaze.

Happy *the foes of broil,*
Who works of *peace* purfue:
The God of peace with fmile
Does his own children view.

 Their godlike frame
 Deferves the name,
 Divinely great
 Is their eftate.

Happy, thrice happy, ye
Who fuffer fcorn and fhame;
Whofe love to truth and me
Endures the teft of flame.

Q

To

To you is giv'n
To fit in heav'n
With me, and fhare
My glory there [z].

※※※※※※※※※※※※※※※※※※

C.

THE CONCLUSION OF A
CHRISTIAN LIFE.

I Fear him not—The king of fears
    Stands ready to difcharge his bow,
No terror in his look appears,
    I bare my bofom to the blow.

'Thou vanquifh'd enemy, my Lord,
    When underneath thy ftroke he fell,
O'ercame thee ; and his pow'rful word
    Thy pow'r againft his friends fhall quell [a].

---

[z] Rev. III. 21.   [a] 1 Corinth. XV. 55—57.

Welcome

Welcome the wound, which fets me free
   From a vain world and finful clay:
'Twill end my dark captivity,
   And give me to immortal day.

My warfare's finifhed [h]. Sins and grief,
   Long has my ftruggle been with you.
O come, faith's long-defir'd relief;
   For ever, grief and fins, adieu.

I haften to my father's home,
   To meet my dear Redeemer there [i].
My naked fpirit fhall not roam,
   In worlds deferted of his care [k].

Nor fhall this flefh I leave behind,
   Lie mould'ring always in the tomb:
Quicken'd by him [l], ere long, refin'd,
   It fhall celeftial life affume [m].

---

[h] 2 Tim. IV. 7.   [i] John XIV. 2, 3. XVII. 24.
Heb. VI. 19, 20.   [k] Acts VII. 59. 2 Tim. I. 12.
[l] John VI. 39.   [m] Philip. III. 20, 21.

        Sweet

Sweet earthly fellowſhips, farewell;
  Belov'd relations, friends belov'd,
With you I muſt no longer dwell:
  How hard to part! my ſoul is mov'd.

But, gracious God, within thy hand
  I truſt them all; their journey guard
Through this diſtemper'd dang'rous land,
  In heav'n's good way to heav'n's reward.

CI.

THE FUNERAL.

IN black proceſſion, ſad and ſlow,
  About the ſtreets the mourners go:
Man comes to make his long abode,
Where darkneſs dwells and worms corrode[n].

---

   [n] Eccleſ. XII. 5.

There

There busy life, there pleasure ends,
And tie of blood, and tie of friends.
There ends probation's hour [o], and there
Virtue's hard strife with sin and care.

Why for vain riches do I toil,
Gath'ring for death a larger spoil [p]?
Why for this dying flesh purvey,
The sinful pleasures of a day [q]?

Why cling so closely to my heart
Kindred and friends? we soon must part!
And wherefore do I waste the span
Of mercy limited to man?

The pious few O let me join,
And with their faith my breath resign;
That their hereafter mine may be,
Ev'n mine their blest eternity [r].

---

[o] Eccles. IX. 10. XI. 3. Heb. IX. 27. [p] Ps. XLIX. 6—9, 17. [q] Rom. XIII. 14. Heb. XI. 25.
[r] Num. XXIII. 10. Prov. XIV. 32. Psal. XXXVII. 37. 2 Corinth. IV. 17, 18.

CII.

THE SEPARATE SOUL OF
A GOOD CHRISTIAN.

WHAT world is this? Where am I brought,
    Stript of my body, but my thought
More clear and vigorous than of late?
Is this the intervening state [s] ?

Eyes

---

[s] The foul of our Saviour went into *Paradife*,
immediately after its feparation from his body. Thither, alfo, on the fame day went the foul of the con-
verted thief. But our Lord afcended not into *heaven*,
till forty days after his refurrection. Surely then
Paradife is not *heaven*, but fome other place in the
univerfe; where the feparate fpirits of good men
dwell together, in joyful expectation of their own
bleffed refurrection and final reward. Compare Luke
XXIII. 43. John xx. 17. Acts I. 3—10. John
XIV. 3. Matt. xxv. 31, 34. *Hades* is fuppofed to
mean the common receptacle of departed fouls, until
the general refurrection. It is conceived to be divided
into two vaft regions, (1) The *lower paradife*, fo
called,

Eyes I have none, nor feet to fteer,
Nor hands to feel, nor ears to hear:
Yet I can reafon as before,
And trace my paft exiftence o'er.

My weeping children, weeping wife,
Ye deareft cares in former life,
All intercourfe with you is o'er;
The home I lov'd, knows me no more.

Cannot unbody'd fouls combine,
And, fpeechlefs, in fweet converfe join?
With mental vifion, lo, I fee
A vaft rejoicing company.

Thefe, furely, are the righteous band
Of fouls, who fojourn in this land,
And is not this unknown abode,
Bleft with the prefence of my God?

---

called, to diftinguifh it from the *upper paradife*, ftyled
by St. Paul *the third heaven* *, into which the juft are
to be received immediately after the general judgement. (2) Gehenna, (hell) named *Tartarus* by St.
Peter †, the place of torment and manfion of wicked
fouls. See Grotius on Luke XXIII. 43.

* 2 Corinth. XII, 2, 4.   † 2 Peter II, 4. in the Original.

Encumber'd now no more with clay,
I've caſt its weakneſſes away [t].
I feel my pow'rs of joy more ſtrong
Than ever did to earth belong.

With raptur'd hope, I wait the morn [u]
When to new life I ſhall be born [w]
By that almighty voice, whoſe found
Shall wake the dead [x] and ſplit the ground;

When I ſhall meet my Saviour-Lord
Coming to finiſh my reward [y];
When I ſhall join his holy train,
And mount to the celeſtial plain [z].

---

[t] Rom. vii. 24, 25.   [u] Pſalm xlix. 14;
[w] Luke xx. 36.   [x] John v. 28, 29.
[y] 2 Theſſ. i. 10.   [z] Matt. xxv. 46. John
xvii. 24.

CIII.

THE MEDIATORIAL KINGDOM
OF JESUS CHRIST.

CELESTIAL Muse, infpire my voice; to fing
Jefus the mediator king [a].
Archangels lowly in his prefence ftand,
In act to fly at his command.

Great legiflator, by fupreme decree,
To Adam's favour'd progeny [b];
On Adam's favour'd offspring he beftow'd
The bleffing of his heav'nly code [c].

The Spirit, Pow'r of fanctitude, receives
Miffion from him [d]; receiving gives
Grace in a rich effufion, to maintain
In human breafts a Saviour's reign.

---

[a] Pfalm cx. 1—4. Matt. xxii. 43, 44. Heb. vii.
20, 21. [b] Pfalm ii. 6. Matt. xvii. 5. Acts
ii. 35. [c] *The gofpel*, Rom. viii. 2.
[d] John xv. 26. xvi. 7—11.

He

He lives, the Mediator [e] lives and pleads,
   For weeping rebels intercedes [f]:
Self-mov'd the Father looks with placid face,
   And yields to rebels his embrace [g].

His Father's pardons he conveys [h], where'er
   Faith offers the repenting tear :
The fulness of his Father's love he sheds,
   Where faith the path of duty treads [i].

Over his flock a watching eye he bends,
   His flock he feeds, his flock defends.
The weak he strengthens, he confirms the strong,
   And gently bears the lambs along [k].

In danger's instant, in temptation's hour,
   His providence exerts its pow'r;
In sorrow's vale, in death's tremendous shade,
   Still present with consoling aid.

———————————

[e] 1 Tim. II. 5.   Heb. VII. 25.
[f] John III. 16. XVI. 26, 27. Rom. v. 8, 10.
[g] 2 Corinth. v. 19. Coloss. I. 21.
[h] Luke XXIV. 47. Acts v. 31.
[i] Heb. v. 9.   [k] Isaiah XL. 11. John X. 11.
Pf. XIII. 1—4.

Mean while, his matchlefs policy prepares,
　　Ye nations; all your great affairs;
And all thy range, O fcience! to fulfill
　　The counfels of redeeming will [l].

He comes, to vindicate his Father's throne;
　　He comes, to glorify his own:
The king defcends in majefty divine,
　　Ten thoufand Seraphs round him fhine [m].

His voice like roaring oceans founds, " Awake
　　Ye dead;" earth, fea, and Hades quake:
The dead before his judgment-feat appear,
　　Their doom the dead and living hear [n].

" Depart, ye curfed, to eternal flame.
　　Ye bleffed, I avow your claim,
The kingdom by my Father's love prepar'd;
　　Me follow to your high reward [o]."

---

[l] Ephef. i. 22. Revel. v. 1—7.
[m] Matt. xvi. 27. xxv. 31. Acts x. 42. Rom. ii. 5.
Jude 14. 2 Theff. i. 6—10. [n] 2 Tim. iv. 1.
1 Theff. iv. 15. Rev. xx. 12.
[o] Matt. xxv. 34, 41.

The

The king precedes, the long refulgent train
    Afcend to his celeftial fane [n] :
The heav'ns roll off; fun, moon, and ftars expire,
    Earth melts in univerfal fire [o].

✳✳✳✳✳✳✳✳✳✳✳✳✳✳✳✳✳✳✳✳✳✳✳✳✳✳✳✳✳✳✳✳

CIV.

THE EVERLASTING GOSPEL.

ETERNAL Gofpel, my unerring guide,
    The worldling's hatred [p], and the fcorn of pride [q],
No vifionary's dream, nor fabling wile,
Frenzy's illufion, or impofture's guile [r];
Mean were thy heralds, but their miffion fure,
The doctrines humbling, and the moral pure,
Benevolence fublime; ftupendous fcheme
God to exalt, and a loft world redeem.

---

[n] *Temple*, that is, *heaven, the true fanctuary*. Heb. VIII. 2. IX. 24. Rev. VII. 15.
[o] 2 Pet. III. 10—12. Rev. XX. 11. 19, 20.   [q] 1 Corinth. I. 22, 23.
[p] John III.   [r] 2 Pet. I. 16.

In

In vain the mighty ftorm'd, the learned ftrove,
Thy truth is ftrong, it iffu'd from above:
Scoffs, chains, and death in all the fhapes of fear
Menac'd in vain; refiftlefs its career:
By wonder-working pow'rs and native charms,
Its fole enticement and its only arms,
From land to land its rapid conquefts fpread,
And joy and beauty on the nations fhed.

O when fhall this divine religion run
In its *full* glory ⁵ with the circling fun?
Come, long foretold, long wifh'd, triumphing day;
Fly, intervening ages, fly away.

'Mong opening clouds, amidft a flood of light,
A man majeftic ᵗ awes the dazzled fight.
High on a courfer ᵘ white as virgin fnow,
He fits; in act to bend a filver bow ʷ;

ˢ Gen. XII. 3. Pfalm II. 8. CX. I. Dan. VII. 13, 14.
ᵗ Jefus Chrift. See Revel. VI. 2.
ᵘ Grotius underftands *the white horfe* to be a fymbol of
the gofpel, in regard to its purity.
ʷ The *bow* may reprefent the vengeance which Jefus
Chrift will inflict on the implacable enemies of his pure
religion. Compare Pfalm XLV. 3, 4, 5.

A golden

A golden crown upon his head behold.
Victor, his name, in characters of Gold,
Flames on a filver crofs his lofty creft ;
And Mercy with foft luftre fparkles on his cheft.

Rome trembling drops her chalice and her rod,
And the freed nations mock her viceroy God [x].
Their ftartled eyes the feed of Ifrael turn
To him their fathers crucify'd, and mourn [y].
Mecca abjures her Ifhmael's fpurious fane [z],
Her prophet faithlefs, and his [a] Koran vain.
India her Viedam [b] burns.   The polifh'd land
Of China owns the Nazarene's command:
Ador'd [c] Confucius is no more divine,
And pagods [d] fall before Jehovah's fhrine.

———————————

[x] 2 Theff. 11. 4.   [y] Zech. xii. 10. Rom.
xi. 24—26. 2 Cor. 111. 13—16.

[z] The Caaba, or temple of Mecca, to which the
Mahometans make pilgrimages.

[a] Commonly called *the Alcoran*, the law of Mahom-
med.   [b] The facred code of the Bramins, in the
Eaft Indies.   [c] A famous Chinefe philofopher.
He had a temple erected to him after his death.

[d] Chinefe idols.

I fee

In Scythian wilds ᵉ, beneath the freezing bear ᶠ,
I fee Immanuel his enfign rear.
ᵍ O'er Lybia's burning plains he fends his name,
And all her fable fons refound his fame.
Salvation with a fwift effulgence beams,
On the vaft weftern world's remote extremes ;
Caciques ʰ and Sachems ʰ lay their axes down :
Barbarian fiercenefs and the favage frown
Melt into focial love, the look humane,
And the mild fpirit of Meffiah's reign.

A new creation fprings, the hallow'd earth
Is fill'd with children of celeftial birth ;
A race divine, to life immortal born ;
Whom God's own virtues with renown adorn;
O times, O manners, innocent and bleft !
Joy to the fwelling womb and milky breaft.
No pirate roves the flood, the trading fail
Securely flies before the fanning gale.

ᵉ Tartary.   ᶠ The moft northern parts of the earth.
ᵍ *Lybia*, i. e. the interior parts of Afric comprehending
The Land of the Negroes.
ʰ Chiefs of the American Indians.

Safe is the travell'd fhore, the pilgrim takes
His fearlefs journey when the morn awakes.
The villages rejoice; th' exulting hind
Eyes his fure harveft waving in the wind.
Nor in the hut alone contentment fings,
But, wond'ring, comes to ftatefmen and to kings.
Cities rejoice; no fons of Belial tear
With bacchanalian roar the midnight air.
Nor lewdnefs prowls at eve, nor villains creep
Through windows in th' unwary hour of fleep.
Juftice her fafces breaks, fierce war his lance,
Order and peace the focial blifs advance:
All kind affections through all hearts extend,
And every man knows every man a friend.
Mefliah reigns, th' Almighty Father fmiles,
Difcord no more his holy mount defiles [i]:
One faith, one hope, the happy nations bind,
The world his Zion, and his fold mankind.

Fly, intervening ages, fly away;
Come long foretold, long wifh'd, triumphing day.

---

[i] Ifaiah xi. 9.

INDEX

I N D E X

O F

F I R S T   L I N E S.

P

INDEX,

D.

E.

F.

G.

H.

9

How

ÍNDEX.

P 2   My

I N D E X.

INDEX.

R.

W.

Y.

F I N I S.